ALSO BY JANE ALISON

The Love-Artist

THE MARRIAGE OF THE SEA

THE

MARRIAGE

OF THE

SEA

JANE ALISON

FARRAR • STRAUS • GIROUX

NEW YORK

Farrar, Straus and Giroux
19 Union Square West, New York 10003

Copyright © 2003 by Jane Alison
Distributed in Canada by Douglas & McIntyre Ltd.
Printed in the United States of America
First edition, 2003

Library of Congress Cataloging-in-Publication Data
Alison, Jane, 1961–
    The marriage of the sea / Jane Alison.— 1st ed.
        p.   cm.
    ISBN 0-374-19941-8
    1. Venice (Italy)—Fiction.   2. New Orleans (La.)—Fiction.   I. Title.
PS3551.L366 M37 2003
813'.6—dc21

                                                                    2002033887

Designed by Jonathan D. Lippincott

www.fsgbooks.com

1   3   5   7   9   10   8   6   4   2

FOR ALEX

THE MARRIAGE OF THE SEA

PROLOGUE

Oswaldo sits on the edge of the bed, slowly stirring sugar into his coffee. Although he has on his slippers and silk pajamas and robe, he's old, and the house is cold and damp, so he tucks his legs back under the covers and gazes out the window, shivering. It's a gray morning, the sea restless and spiteful, not the bright smooth jade for which it's famous. He can hear it lapping against the walls, and he knows that if he gets out of bed, walks down the hall, and looks over the balustrade at the *piano terreno*, he'll see puddles all over the floor, gleaming like fat slugs in the garden. And to think that the sea was once so kind to this city! Once she bore it the riches of the world and protected it with a liquid wall, but now she has become the enemy. Outside the window, water sloshes against a wooden pile in the canal, wearing it away, nudging it loose from the slippery mud. Oswaldo puts down his cup, pulls up the covers, and runs his tongue along his teeth, fretting that they have become so thin. Thin, yes, and then they'll fall out, and he'll have nothing but slick old gums. How has it gotten so *late* in his life? He is not ready for this. Because despite all that he's seen and had and done, he still wants—

He gets out of bed and paces, tugging at the tips of his long gray moustache. He has everything, after all: palazzo, silk socks, the Fondazione. Yet despite his wealth, he feels so reduced. Not in his means, though: in his substance. His hair, skin, nails, and bone are all thinning and turning brittle, and there's only a trickle of blood in his veins, traveling its weary rounds. Like an hourglass, a klepsydra: he pictures it, the water thief, water running out with time, although here (another surge sloshes against a pile)—here water itself is the thief. He walks down the hall, and glancing over the banister, finds what he expected. The sea keeps creeping in.

Disgruntled, Oswaldo goes back to bed. He rings the bell for a fresh espresso, peers out into the fog, and longs for he does not know what.

It's a rainy morning in London, and Max, who always wakes with a jolt at five, has been running up and down between his flat and the cellar for more than two hours, arms full of boxes and old sacks and books. His face is long, narrow, prematurely lined, and his hair—gold-white—springs in little gossamer curls. The flat around him is all tea chests, junk, as he's always had a weakness for broken things that once were fantastical: a silver pocket nutmeg grinder, a moth-eaten reproduction of the famous fur teacup. For hours he's been making piles, trying to decide what should stay and what should go; suddenly he sneezes, dropping a dusty book, one leg kicking out dramatically. He blows his nose and, all at once worn out, falls into a chair. There he shuts his eyes and lets himself float, listening to the rain. As he relaxes, his mouth—so mobile just a moment before as he muttered and whistled, sorting—drops into a sad, fallen shape. Then his mind cannot help but wander, as it has wandered for years, to the ghostly flat upstairs.

Once this flat had access to that one; both couples left their doors open, and the women even decorated the hallway between so that it seemed one big jolly house. But that place, like its tenants, was far slyer and more elegant than this, music and martinis traveling up and down nightly, and of course that wasn't all. Now, in the dim light and gentle rain, Max can still, after years, hear his wife's voice falling softly from upstairs, feel that terrible information falling upon him like snow.

He opens his eyes and sits up, setting both feet smartly on the floor. He is not going to think about *that*. The others have all moved away since then, the locks have long been changed, and Therese has long since learned to fend for herself—although even that thought makes his heart ache with pity.

But now he is going himself.

Max sits up straight and looks out like a ship captain at all the tea chests and boxes, at his plane ticket balanced with virtuosity upon a little structure of pencils on the mantel, at his passport triumphantly displayed atop that. Going! He sees the new woman upon whom he has fixed himself, although he considers her more *femme* than woman. His proposal to her was not altogether a *proposal*—more a statement, an idea, phrased in such a way that acknowledged she would of course need time, need to think. And certainly he's not going to New Orleans just for her; thank heavens there are the requirements of life to prevent that sort of danger. No, he has a new position, temporary and honorific: he is to be the first occupant of a new chair in the History of Food. Surely the place will yield wonders: fascinating near fossils of foods, baroque, fanciful, ludic. So it is altogether apt that he should go; it isn't foolish at all. And he knows that all those signs—(1) that unnerving, unmistakable excitement when, having flown over to discuss the position last fall, he first met *la femme* (a staged extravaganza had been planned to entice him, and she was the one who executed such things), followed by (2) what he could only call an enchantment (Max was hardly able to see, his water-blue eyes astonished after every blink to find her still there); (3) her watching him slyly from the corner of her eye as she took him to the city's secret places, all the while teasing him out like a winkle from its shell; and finally, over the past few months, (4) the extraordinary series of hand-collaged cards that she's sent him (bikinied girls, alligators, Black Lagoon) and (5) those precious, precious late-night phone calls, her silvery voice in his electrified ear—he knows that none of these promise a thing. Because of course he understands: she'll need time.

Good heavens, she knows so very little! Just his teeth that would not stop smiling, and his hand that flew in alarm toward her shoulder each time she risked the perils of a street. *Grac*ious, Maximilian, she had said lazily, allowing herself to be steered, aren't you courtliness itself? The look her amused eye left upon his hand made his fingers tingle, and he controlled them with his thumb.

Max turns his hand over and looks at his palm as if he's never seen it before. *Hers* he knows by heart, though, for it is strangely lineless. She'd flaunted it at Napoleon's or somewhere on only the fifth day, teasing that she had no love line. . . . But he seized the opportunity, seized her hand, and at the sheer contact smiled so violently he almost burst from his skin as he said—what did he say? *With a nice sharp knife I could fix that!* At which she looked both delighted and shocked and laughed with a sound like glass smashing, before simply saying, Well, *well*!

So now—what else can Max do? Life has long since moved out of this flat; perhaps it's over there. So he is going, to New Orleans. And here is the fax he will send her, penned in his exuberant, looping hand. *My most entrancing L,* he's written, but, given her own teasing letters, why not? *What I should like to propose—*

He decided last week not to telephone. He's already accepted the position, taken temporary leave.

A flash fills the room and disappears, silent like heat lightning. He glances out the window in time to see a red glimmer reflected in the watery street, the soundless ambulance disappearing.

Max turns back to the room, all the boxes, and goes over to the desk, looks once more at the letter. He feeds in the sheet, dials her number, waits without breathing throughout the three, four rings, and then hears her recorded voice, a voice that always seems like light or the sheen of a metal. He listens to it, tapping his tongue against his teeth. The paper winds slowly through, comes out, and the machine goes still. It's done. Soon the men from Sea & Air will take away his crates, and he will leave.

At the same time, across the Atlantic in granite New York, Lachlan skids down the stairwell, shaken but free, and bursts out into the glorious cold night. The air is sharp, trash flying along Grand Street. He throws his scarf around his unshaven neck, shoves his hands in his pockets, and starts whistling, then, realizing he shouldn't whistle so near, lowers his head and hurries. Free!

Vera didn't take it well. But why should she? Lach would hate to be in her position, just hate it; he can't think of anything worse. He shudders, imagining someone like himself coming in, with soft, remorseful smiles. . . . He feels all nerves and guilty, yet *free*, and somehow it's like his clothes, paint-spattered, expensive: himself.

Oh god, I'm sorry, he'd said.

She'd looked at him. What?

It's just that I can't help it, he'd said.

At that she had started to laugh.

He's across the street now, facing the wind, halfway down the block. Lach tramps when he walks, head forward, Neanderthal, neither tall nor short but just right for most women, he long ago discovered. They even liked the slightly female softness of his body, the good-natured badness of his puppy dog ways, his head rubbing against their petting hands while his eyes looked around cheerily for others. Cab or train? Oh, it's late, and he is so wonderfully rich; just today Arn sold another piece! And of course Francesca is waiting. Lach blinks the soot from his watering eyes, then stops, astounded, in the middle of the street. Are his eyes actually watering with *emotion*?

He can't altogether understand this thing that seems to happen to him. He just wakes up startled to find himself where he is, in bed beside a woman, and even though she's a woman he's woken up with for ages, suddenly it's as if a mistake has been made, he has on the wrong clothes or even the wrong name, and what he must do at once is flee. He feels terrible whenever this happens, just terrible.

Ah, Vera, he thinks, and is wan and wrenched, seeing again her tearing eyes, her large, trembling, blood-filled lips. But then he thinks *Francesca*, and at once he can smell her golden skin. And now, it's true: he can go back with her to Venice, to his wonderful, ruined pink house.

Her name? Vera had said.

Lach had stared miserably at the wall.

Her *name*!

So he told her, and may even, he is sorry to think, have given the doorjamb an affectionate squeeze.

Francesca, she repeated, tasting it slowly. Venetian? You met her in Venice? In the last two *months*?

Milanese, actually, he answered. But yes.

Lach takes out a cigarette and lights it, his long black coat blowing, the flame of the match giving a blanched starkness to his frog lips, thick blond brows, dangling strands of hair. His face is crumpled, eyes crinkled, his teeth the teeth of a dissolute. He exhales, feels the exhalation become a sigh, and turns back to look at the building where for several years he and Vera happily, and then not so happily, lived. How many years has it been, in fact? He rubs his eyes; he can't remember. Everything seems to be *blurred* somehow. Ah, Vera, he thinks. How did this happen? Her black horse hair, her green-veined wrists, her magnificent blossomy body. She'd always been so intense, reserved. Did he ruin her? He'd consumed her from the moment she turned up in his studio, so willing and talented! Well, he thinks, maybe not so talented. Actually, just now he can't recall. He knits his brows and sees her again as she was that first night, knees bent and bum up on his paint-crusted table as headlights streamed over the walls. How did these things fall apart?

Lach draws pensively on his cigarette. Of course what he has told her is that he needs time. Which isn't altogether a lie, is it? He always does things so rashly. Just give me time! he'd sobbed in the middle of it all, standing in front of her wet-faced like a baby. But still: his traveling shoes were on, as he says, and what else could he do? He must fly.

Exactly how much time? she'd said.

I don't know. Oh god, he said, loving two women—

At that she turned white, turned away.

Lach looks back again at the studio windows, a wringing in his chest. When he left, she was standing perfectly still, staring at the wall. She actually threw him against it! He's forgotten this until now: how her pale teeth, the shadows under her eyes, not a word but a cold breath like frost from her mouth—how all of it moved intently toward him, and the next thing he knew he was staggering, slamming into the wall. He slumped to the floor, shocked, and looked up at her without a word, as she looked, just as shocked, down at him. Then she ran to the bathroom and vomited.

She is scary, he thinks. She's *dangerous*. Lach exhales in a rush, drops the cigarette and grinds it out with a ruined shoe, flings the scarf again around his neck, and hurries on. He's sick of New York. He wants to be safe in his little pink house in Venice; he can smell its old floorboards, see the fabled watery light. He stops at the corner, where the cross signal is broken—DON'T ALK, DON'T ALK—and waves his hand for a cab.

Far to the south, in a city as crescent-shaped and riven as Venice, on the second floor of an old yellow house, Anton is kneeling beside his wife, Josephine, drawing on her as she sleeps. His body is naked and awkwardly long as he bends over her, making hearts with arrows, his black hair and the shadows from his fine, arched nose a little blue in the light; the hand that draws trembles slightly. He can't sleep from worry, from excitement. Most of his things are already packed—his Lorenzetti, maps, mechanical pencils, Mayline, camera, and books—but as he was gathering his Prismacolors and markers, he saw her lying there, sheet shoved away in a dream, and decided to draw her a message. It's become a ritual between them: at first just a note by the bed, then a tiny heart drawn stealthily on her leg, never as baroque as this. But why not? He'll be away for two months. The red felt-tip glides along her ribs as he draws skulls and crossbones, cartoons. The smell of live oak, old and green, floats in through the window.

At Josephine's stomach Anton pauses, leaning on his elbows, his breath falling in time with hers. Such an orchid, this Josephine, skinny and stemmy but voluptuous, weighted by her difficult head and all that tangled red hair. He places a long hand upon her stomach—covering so much of it, his hand is so large—and can't decide whether to do it or not, but then he can't resist. He draws a round head with a curling lock of hair, a little body, pudgy arms, a pair of kicking legs: a baby, part Kewpie, part putto.

Anton raises himself, disoriented. Just eleven o'clock: only a few hours until the cab comes. He and Josephine have rarely been apart in three years, and when they have, never for more than a weekend, with phone calls twice a day. For a moment he's upset that she sleeps. But when she sleeps, she does so obstinately; it's the only thing, he sometimes thinks, she really wants to do. Which is how he came to draw the little notes to begin with. *Sleeping Josephine, I've gone to work, although I love you more than ever.* He gazes down at his red baby, watches it rise and fall, then crouches again and adds several halo rays to its head. For it will be an immaculate baby. . . . Anton is still mortified at the thought, the way he is so often mortified, a pall dropping over his wide, graceful shoulders and his staring eyes. With an effort he shrugs it away; it does not matter at all what kind of baby it is, just as long as there is one.

He draws his finger from the little kicking foot he's drawn down Josephine's body, lifting his hand politely away at the dark curls and landing again at her knee. Why doesn't she wake up, wait with him until he's gone! He feels sick, unsteady. But packed already in a jeweler's felt sack, with his cuff links and antique compass, is the spool of ribbon on which he carefully recorded Josephine three years ago, like a pilgrim taking the measure of Hagia Sophia. From the end of the ribbon to point one is the distance from Josephine's chin to her eyes; from there to point two is the unfathomable space between earlobes; from there to point three is the span of her hand, measured from the shape of warmth left on his leg, where it had lingered one day as he drove.

Anton's own hand is stained with red ink, and it trembles, it always trembles. Often he wishes it would not give him away so quickly; he's been trying to turn that tremble, in his renderings and drawings, into a distinctive rippling line expressing the energy and excitement he so terribly feels. He forces his hand to be still now and looks at it in the moonlight, one finger encircled by a band of white gold, such precious proof of solidity, of substance. And this hand has just secured for him the position that will transport him briefly to another world, a world where something must happen, it has two months to happen, so that then he'll be able to return to Josephine and say to her, We will be fine.

There's a sudden flash of heat lightning, and the bedroom walls, Anton's bags, the bed—everything is lit. He stares down at what he's done to her, horrified. What was he thinking? He hurries to the bathroom to wet a tissue and tries to wipe the awful baby away, but it only smears, larger and worse. Finally there's nothing to do but write an apology on her hand. He looks at her then, sleeping. He gets up and moves silently about the apartment, gathering the rest of his things.

Downtown, in a small raised cottage at the edge of the French Quarter with its old, straight streets, Lucinde is in her favorite room, the one with the clawfoot bathtub and the chimney that's been turned into a light shaft. She's getting undressed with one hand and holding the phone with the other while she keeps an eye on the water that rises slowly in the tub.

"My god, my god," Lucinde murmurs. She's called Vera to check the dates in Venice, only to discover that she has stepped

into a disaster. Really, though, she's not so surprised; from Lachlan, who would have expected anything else?

"Yes," she says, "oh, poor thing, I know."

She realizes as she listens that there is a slightly new twist this
time: Venice. She smiles with distaste. "Awful," she says, "awful.
Of course, he forgot you applied. It's absolutely intolerable. But
you know, you won it, so you're going. Yes"—she is firm—"oh
yes. And I'll be there at least one week, with Oswaldo. Don't
worry. We'll do something. Please don't worry." When the water
is just a hand span from the rim, she makes a gentle exit.

Dropping her clothes to the floor, Lucinde has just put one
foot in the bath when the telephone rings. With her foot slightly
scalding, she waits for the message, her tall, soft body in the mirror like a painting, steam hovering about it, rosy hues; it's a body
like that of a very large child, although few people know this. After three rings the letter starts to scroll out, and when it falls free
and curls, she limps over.

As Lucinde reads her eyebrows rise. She laughs then, nervous,
the paper sticking to her fingertips, and quickly shakes it free.
Noises and voices come in from the street, and she glances at the
windows, although she knows that they and the doors are locked.
But her white walls are only painted to look like stone: never,
never thick enough. She touches her ears, which seem to be ringing, and feels a little dizzy, the steam on her skin transformed to
sweat. Having folded the letter in half lengthwise, she smooths
the crease with the side of her hand. But she's not sure what to do
with the letter; after a moment she slides it under the phone.
Then she goes back to the bath and steps in.

So, you actually meant it.

Well, *well*.

But you don't even know me.

Lucinde sinks, her body bumping on the porcelain bottom of the tub, and gazes up at the light shaft she loves. She holds her wet hands before her and ponders them: so very familiar, so terribly familiar, as familiar, perhaps, as the bars of a cage. She turns them around, looking at their plump smoothness, their lack of lines, and wonders.

Perhaps, she thinks, perhaps—

Abruptly she climbs from the tub and goes back to the telephone, dripping. Seven hours' difference, so it's only six-thirty in the morning for him, but he won't mind if she calls; he'll already be having his second coffee. She dials and listens to the foreign ring, sees it traveling through underwater cables.

"Pronto?" His voice is rough, as if unused to talking.

"Oswaldo," Lucinde says, and realizes that she's whispering, as if someone might hear through the faux-stone walls or might have slipped in through the cracks, through the light shaft. She straightens and laughs. "Oh, Oswaldo," she says.

"Lucinde. What is it? Now what have you done? Don't tell me you are not coming."

"No," she says. "Actually, I was wondering, Oswaldo, could I come a little early?"

Max landed in New Orleans like a sprinter. His cab barreled over the toxic empty highway into town, the battered streets and battered sidewalks and battered, crooked houses. He'd chosen the most romantic hotel, just beyond the Garden District, lopsided and seedy. Once he'd checked in he ran up the staircase, noting with delight the stained glass promise in the window: *Let my beloved come into his garden and eat his pleasant fruits!* Then he had barely put down his bag, barely phoned Sea & Air to provide a temporary number (should his fur teacup and cookbooks and secondhand Paul Smiths be lost at sea in their nailed, stamped crates), before he washed his hands, looked at his teeth, tried to order his fly-away ringlets, paced once up and down the room, lifted the receiver, and dialed. He did it standing, bursting from his body, his mouth stretched in the same wide smile that had stretched it inanely that whole wondrous week. And there, miraculously, she was.

"Well!" she said, slowly but with an unmistakable exclamation mark. Which meant—? "So, Maximilian, you're actually here."

Yes, yes, he tried not to babble, here I am, here I am, for you! He sat down on the bed, but one leg continued to jog and bounce so he clapped a hand heavily upon it.

"We'll have to see each other, then, won't we?" she said.

Which meant—? Max stood up again. His mouth was open in a half-smile, poised to say the next giddy thing, but it went dry that way as, at her end, there was a sudden noise and her voice changed.

"Oh dear, I've got to run. Money's calling, can't be resisted. Call me back in a couple of hours."

Max hung up, suddenly vague, and lay down, or rather unfolded, on the bed. He could hear people out on the porch downstairs. With one eye he studied the floor, which sloped. Perhaps he could smell margaritas from here. Suddenly he sneezed the way he always did, as if the sneeze had erupted from deep in the ground and shaken his whole body with force; he blew his nose noisily and shut his eyes, recovering.

Thick air, very thick air you could almost see hanging—but better than London, certainly. Max looked at his watch and noticed that he had not yet adjusted it. This took some seconds. He got up and lifted the rotting window higher and looked out. The place seemed lazy, all those things it was famed for: Spanish moss, crumbling columns. A hum of voices, a certain smell— electricity, he realized, from the streetcar rattling by. Unknown plants all over. Reluctantly he went out for a walk.

When he came back, he paced around the room a few minutes, whistling between his teeth, then arched, touched his toes, and called her again. No answer. He felt sick and lay down once more on the bed. He opened the *Times Literary Supplement*, which, folded, he'd banged upon his knee almost the entire Virgin Air flight, and now managed with it to consume more than an hour, until at last it was again time to call.

She had changed her recording, just for him, which had a mixed effect. He was to call tomorrow, her voice said, so sorry she didn't have his number, so *rude* to make him keep calling.

Now Max had an entire night. He drank two exceptionally salty margaritas on the porch downstairs, and thought of that island somewhere nearby that was supposed to be made of salt, and watched the news, which seemed very American. He ate not the best sample of red beans and rice. For a time he studied the different bottles of hot sauce, comparing ingredients and quantities of sugar and making a few notes about peppers; briefly but vividly he thought about how the heat trickled from the pepper's veins to its seeds, and how when people said pepper, most often they confused the capsicum with *Piper nigrum* itself, and how for true pepper (by which he meant *Piper nigrum*) men had once sailed all the seas, and how, in contrast, the flavor of paprika disappeared so quickly, poor little fugitive spice. Finally he trudged upstairs, fell asleep, and, without knowing it, snored violently.

The next morning Max was all fresh and shaven at seven o'clock, ready to grapple bulls, all bright smile. And when he dialed her number, there it was, her live voice!

"I'm so sorry, darling," she said. "I'm afraid we've missed. I'm leaving this afternoon for a meeting in New York, and then I'm on to Venice."

"Ahh." A single note was breathed from him, an involuntary expiration, and without wishing it at all, he felt his mouth fall into that sad shape, that ghost from the old flat upstairs.

But very well. He was here. She'd be back. Patience he'd always had.

A few blocks away from Max's hotel, across Saint Charles and down toward the river, Josephine slipped on a paper robe and stood in the curtained dressing room, wondering about her socks. She decided to keep them on.

"What a shame about your husband," said Doctor Gare as she climbed onto the table. He rolled toward her on a stool, pulled on his gloves, and smiled with his very red lips and walleyes.

"Yes," she agreed. "Still, Venice."

Doctor Gare's nurse looked up from over her tubes.

"How true," said Doctor Gare. "Who could resist Venice?"

He switched on the lamp and pulled a prophylactic over the device with a taut little snap. "Lie back, please," he said cheerily, so Josephine lay back on the table and opened her legs with the usual dismay, staring up at the poster of Hawaii on the ceiling.

Today, after a year of failure, she was entering what Doctor Gare liked to call the artificial domain, and she couldn't help but picture him as its keeper, holding a ring of gold keys. She and Anton had decided only last month, and since then she had taken pills every morning, and they'd waited and watched until the moment was ripe. But the timing of everything went off, and Anton needed to fly to Venice before they'd actually done it. No matter! Doctor Gare had cried; that's what makes this domain so marvelous. You simply leave us your sample, and then you're free to go and join a crusade if you like. We've got everything we need right here, he said as he waved the specimen jar.

The whole thing embarrassed both Anton and Josephine. Not only the humiliating fact itself, but the language, the devices, the money. Yet after the first dull surprise of failure, and all the bloodlettings and probings that had turned up nothing, and then the months of plotting Josephine's temperature upon chart after chart taped to the bedroom walls, the relentless red line wavering around them, it seemed like the thing to do, and a thing to do fast before the insurance policy changed in the spring. Doctor Gare had been pleased with their decision. He didn't smile exactly, but the way the sun came in behind him, lighting his fine, floating hair, lent him a contented divinity. He rubbed his fingers together and leaned forward, his hands white, hair white, smock white, Josephine's own face reflected thin and pale amid her flaming hair in his glasses. But you know, he'd said brightly, of course this still may not solve the problem. There is always the ten to fifteen percent of those for whom we never know what's wrong!

Well, at any rate, wrong with *her.*

Josephine studied the tropical waterfall overhead and dug her fingertip into her left temple as Doctor Gare slid the device inside her; she glanced down to see him staring at the screen as obscure constellations appeared. He'd had his first look for follicles last July. What we are looking for, he'd said, is black holes. Not actual black holes of course, just what they remind me of, a certain empty density, if you know what I mean . . . A follicle, where an egg is maturing. Might be maturing, anyway, we don't know, there might of course be nothing inside. Wonderful! he'd said then, spinning back on his stool. You've got seven! She'd felt rich, laden, like a real woman, but even with seven eggs it still hadn't worked. Then, the next time, in September, there had been only four.

He rolled back now and blinked brightly. "Two."

Josephine leaned up on her elbows. "Two?"

"Not quite a quorum, it's true, but enough."

"Really?"

"Of course! Of course."

"All right," she said, and lay back down, digging her fingertip now into her right temple.

Seven, four, two.

"Two?" she said again, lifting her head. "Is that really enough?"

His walleyes peered up through her bare legs. "For this? Oh yes," he said, "oh yes. As you know, we need only one." And at that he pried her open with his clamp.

She put two cold fingertips on each of her eyelids. After a few minutes she felt a little stab, and Doctor Gare cried to his nurse, "I'm in!" She handed him a glass and a slender long tube.

"Off we go," he said. "Let's wish our crusader the best!"

Then he fed the stuff in, the sacred moment came, Josephine felt nothing, the moment passed.

Doctor Gare looked at her beneficently a few seconds before rolling away on his stool. "Positive thoughts!" he said, peeling the gloves from his hands. "Just lie there for a while. Relax."

Then he patted her hot head and left the room, and the nurse switched off the light and followed him. Josephine lay perfectly still, not breathing, as the sound of traffic drifted in from the street.

The apartment Anton had arranged to sublet belonged to an art historian on leave. It was on the second floor of a building at the bottommost tip of Venice and had a rounded terrace, from which Anton could look through the pines and cypresses of the park out to the lagoon and all the way to the Lido, and he could not believe his luck to be in such a building, a building so much like a ship.

He had been there with his students for just eight days and had already marched them not only to the more obvious places but to Scarpa's museum and the new housing projects on Cannareggio and the Giudecca; he'd taken them to Vicenza on Wednesday and to Verona on Friday, and today they were going to Padova. As he walked through the cool, hazy morning air, Anton imagined his route from above as on an antique map (tinted olive, aqua, and red, with tiny rippling waves of the lagoon drawn in) and actually allowed himself to *see* himself striding across the fabulous city as architects had done for centuries: the top of his dark head; his long legs moving purposefully in their trousers; black drawing book clamped under his arm; pavement rocking and water slapping in his wake.

Anton walked a deliberately circuitous route, pleased to know his way so well, never to pause baffled at a corner, to look as though he might actually belong here. From the bottom of the island he headed through the straight zones of new housing and up to Via Garibaldi, to real life, the paper. He stopped for a coffee where he always stopped, put one polished shoe on the brass rail, and produced the formula—*Buon giorno, buon giorno, macchiato, si!*—all of it gliding convincingly along. Then, with the coffee shot back, the lire slapped down, up familiar Garibaldi he strode until he reached . . . the milky jade water, the light! Anton's heart nearly flew from his chest, again, as it nearly flew each morning. San Giorgio, the marina, and the Dogana—*Salute!*

Was that his boat already? Coming or going? His throat constricted, and he hurried over the pavement, clattered along the ramp, but before reaching the boat he saw with horror the young man undo the rope and the water begin to churn, and he sprang and leapt over the growing green gap, feeling himself now a flapping black scarecrow, bones in an old man's coat, big shoes, but miraculously he landed on deck. The iron gate slid shut behind him, and the vaporetto shuddered and barged into the lagoon.

Three of his students were huddled by the cabin. They mouthed wry congratulations at his leap; he nodded, still rattled, and went inside the cabin. He took a seat and busily opened his black book, whose pages were plastered with the sheets of a calendar, letters, cards, train and museum tickets, all intervening spaces covered with diagrams and drawings and notes; in his trembling hand were sketches of tiny façades and plans, sections of palazzi from mud to golden crowns, as well as Minoletti's pool and villa on the lake, the stilted town in Key Biscayne, the steamboat houses below the levee. Water architecture: why he was here. It was a one-year post, the first half last spring in New Orleans and the rest of it, the dessert, here; he'd begun making excited notes the moment they offered the job, because imagine the possibilities: Le Flottant and Venice itself! Normally he'd need a grant to be here, but now he was official, moving about authoritatively within the mantle of a position. He'd already taken dozens of rolls of film and blocked out, at night, a first drawing. It would all become at least one article and, he hoped, an exhibit, plus catalogue, which would surely—added to his other articles and his published, if not built, designs—help him finally get somewhere.

At any rate, something must happen. Anton had exactly two months to find himself something else, something solid. A permanent position or else a project, something conspicuous, concrete. He was nearly forty, and he just could not keep floating like this. Especially now, with Josephine.

He looked down at his book. If his students were all at the station in time, they'd be in Padova by nine-twenty. First the Arena Chapel, next the Eremitani, then a straight march to Sant' Antonio, over to the Basilica and the Salone, a stop at the Caffè Pedrocchi, finishing up at the anatomical theater, by which point they'd be exhausted.

The vaporetto chugged along, banging at the docks; he wiped the window and gazed out, then looked back at his book, his calendar, to a few days before. At the moment when Josephine was to be lying on Doctor Gare's table (her appointment was at ten in the morning so five in the afternoon for him), Anton had made a point of being back in the apartment at the bottom of Venice and sitting still, penitent, alone. He had stared down at the cold tiled floor and, feeling lonely and strange and far away, found himself looking in the mirror for company. His long legs were crossed, his hands latched around the knee, his shoes gleaming in the dimness, the bluish shadow from his fine nose falling off-kilter and somewhat severe—all of it, he realized with wonder, *elegant*. Uncrossing his legs, he turned away from the mirror and concentrated on Josephine, far away. He did not like to think about

Doctor Gare busy between her legs but took comfort from the thought of the rubber gloves and thick glasses. He imagined those tiny parts of his own self at that moment in a tube, in a pipe, but this made his cheeks burn, so he shut his eyes and with an effort transformed the whole scenario: the fine pipe became the beam of light falling in the window, and Doctor Gare's face became the face watching benignly from luminous clouds. At five-thirty Anton decided it was probably all over, so he got up, took his black book from his satchel, and on that day on the calendar drew a little star. On each of the days since, he had drawn a small open circle in the morning, and if the day ended without bad news, he'd carefully colored in the little circle; this seemed somehow to reinforce the days, to reinforce the prospects. He was not quite consciously glad he didn't have an answering machine, glad his mobile didn't work, glad there was the problem with time zones. Because at any moment the phone could ring, and there she'd be with that terrible low laugh, standing (he knew) with her pants kicked off, squeezing her eyes shut, in tears.

Yet he could actually cup his hands and *feel* the baby now!

Anton shifted in his seat and fixed his eyes on the passing façades of rose marble and Istrian stone, the edge of green water moving sinuously along the side of the embankment. A plastic bottle floated from a canal, slowly making its way from the shadows out to the lagoon, nudging against a stray leaf of lettuce. He watched the bottle bob and turn gently, rolling in the water. Then, with no warning, it transformed. Turning in the light, it became again that old, old image. The sodden white shirt, the floating tie, the drowned hand still holding a cigarette.

Anton's eyes were dry; he blinked. The plastic bottle became itself. He stared a moment longer, until he was gazing at his own reflection in the window: the nervous cobalt eyes, the excitable mouth, the fine gray coat, the gold watch. He trembled with a sudden gust of defiance and ran a hand through his hair.

A barge plowed by, and, as he saw it, Anton suddenly thought of Rossi's floating theater, seeing again the extraordinary building floating down the canal. How could he only just now remember it? Quickly he made a diagram right where his hand was, in November.

When he reached the *ferrovia*, a collection of students lounged on the steps, the same two once again missing. He flicked an impatient hand, and the students followed him up the steps to the station as flecks of metal might a magnet—which he could actually feel at his heels—until all of a sudden, unable to resist, he stopped in his tracks, making the students stagger and stumble, and turned to cast a punishing look at the two who now came running, giggling, over the bridge.

Along the canal and across the lagoon, in the small pink house by the church of the Redentore, Lach was just getting up. He climbed down the ladder from the attic bedroom, naked but for thick wool socks, his eyes stuck with sleep, belly gently rounded, pale penis dangling from its soft nest of blond hair. The house was square, partly ruined, and only the attic and the first floor aboveground (which he now reached) were inhabitable. Sweet little house! The floorboards were ancient, polished smooth; three windows looked west to the Redentore itself, another looked east down the embankment, and the two at the front looked over the water, down toward the Salute. He adored even the house's ruin, some of which he would definitely have the architect preserve. Here and there on the walls were the chalk markings he'd made only last summer, when he had run around the place doing the math, realizing that, what with his last show's selling out, he could actually buy it. Buy the little pink house by the Redentore! A house on the Giudecca island, in Venice! Lach rubbed his eyes, stretched lazily, and pulled the cord to the old velvet curtains so that they parted in billows of dust, revealing the tossing green water, the famous skyline. *Miràcolo!* A vaporetto plowed by, and he bobbed back and forth on his heels; the church bells began to ring.

Humming, Lach tramped into the kitchen. He spooned coffee into the machine, spilled, wiped it to the floor with the side of his hand. When the flame was lit, he ran down to the ground floor and cracked the door just enough to let in the ozone sea smell of Venice and allow a paint-spattered hand to fumble for the mail.

He was a little dizzy as he climbed back up the dark stairs; he liked grappa much too much and really would drink less, starting today. So what was there: an invitation to an opening somewhere, much too far to bother with; a magazine he ought to cancel one day, he could not even remember subscribing; a phone bill he just wouldn't look at. He noticed now the answering machine blinking. Yes, last night, sometime or other, the phone had been ringing, hadn't it? He pushed the button, but when he heard Vera's voice, a little cage latched around his heart.

"Lach." Her voice was high, slipping out like gas from a bottle. "Pick up if you're there, please. Lach." She paused, and just hearing her breath up close in the phone he winced with the whole sense of her, abandoned. She cleared her throat and went on. "Well. As you might remember, I applied for a prize from the foundation to spend a few months in Venice. The idea was that I would have my own accommodations, that being true at the time. I got the prize. I arrive November fifteenth and will be there until March. I understand your desire not to see me"—she paused again, coughed—"et cetera, but clearly we should talk about it. Call."

Lach rewound the message, the fact winding into his mind, in pictures.

Just what was she doing?

He looked up, looked around, rubbed his nose with his fist. Light was falling in the window, the famous watery light he had come for, falling upon the floorboards, the thin Oriental, the moss-green velvet antique sofa and cherry chairs delicate as does, upon the swaths of color he'd painted, testing gleefully, in spots around the room. He sat on the sofa. There was a sputtering in the kitchen.

Back in the main room, with his coffee, he paced. He sat again and leaned his elbows on his knees and tried to concentrate. He just couldn't remember her applying. He could not remember it at all. And shouldn't he? They would have talked about it. Of course they would have. He'd have needed to write her a letter of recommendation.

Or did he?

He couldn't remember. He could never remember anything. He would never drink grappa again.

He took a sip of his coffee. It was burnt.

He shook his head quickly at the wall. Well, maybe she *had* applied. Maybe he'd even written! Which of course he should have done. But still, he felt unclean, apprehensive.

Because wouldn't you think she'd want to put the fellowship off for a while? Rather than create this *unpleasant* situation? You could always do that. He knew for certain that the foundation would let her, because he'd had the same prize eleven years ago, when everything was just beginning. To put the thing off would be so much more natural! Time, he had said; didn't she understand? That had been the idea. Time *apart*. And now she was coming to Venice?

Well, of course. He flung himself back, crossed his plump bare legs. Of course, she was pursuing.

A little wave of something went through him. Disgust, as for something he could actually smell, and the faintest, foulest pleasure.

Immediately he was ashamed. You've done enough damage, he scolded himself. Look at the position you've put her in! You should have pity, tenderness, compassion, he thought, and he hummed the words as he made fresh coffee to carry carefully up the ladder to Francesca's slumbering golden form.

But what if she wanted to stay in the house? She would. Of course she would!

Well, he would have to let her. It was the least he could do: appeasement, atonement. He felt better at once.

That afternoon Lach called New York. As he heard the familiar rings far away, he could see the loft as it had been the night he left, the sickly light, that shocking long crack in the plaster wall where Vera had thrown him, Vera herself standing before it. Imagine how he once had loved all those things! The only place he'd wanted to be! Only a month before, he'd been on the same phone Vera now was reaching for, curled secretively around the receiver, talking to Francesca all the way over here, when Vera had walked dangerously near him, and he'd coughed, felt himself in a mirror. *But what will I do about Vera?* he'd been whispering. Sickening if she'd heard.

"I want to stay in the house," Vera said now, before they'd even had pleasantries. Her voice alarmed him, jolting like electricity. "It's embarrassing if I can't," she said.

"Yes," he said. "Certainly, yes." He was able to modulate his voice. "Sure, you can stay in the house." He glanced over at the narrow green eyes of Francesca as she watched from the velvet couch. He had hurried around when they first arrived, packing away traces and pictures of Vera.

"So when are you coming?" he asked.

"What?"

"When are you coming to Venice?"

"November fifteenth. I said."

"So shall I—"

"No, I still have a key."

"Oh well," he said afterward to Francesca, who shrugged her sculptural shoulders. "There wasn't any choice, was there? What else could we do?" Lach stood with his hands deep in his corduroy pockets, looking sadly around. He sighed, smiled. They'd just go back to Francesca's dark place behind the church of San Zaccaria—thank god he still had a lease on the studio by the boathouse—and he'd postpone the renovations to the house.

Oswaldo looked in at the guest room, then turned to gaze after his housekeeper disappearing down the hall through shafts of dust. Only the barest minimum, he thought, stepping into the room and straightening the carpet with the toe of his shoe. Although at least the sheets were starched and ironed, and the silver water jug was on the bedside table, and the pillows were properly plumped. But flowers? The old dresser stood plain with its tarnished, tilted mirror and coffee-stained lace. The woman never thought of flowers. He supposed he would have to buy them himself. He wondered what would be available in November, then recalled that everything was always available now, fruit and flowers all year.

But Lucinde would not even be here until tomorrow morning! He did not know what to do until then.

Oswaldo sat down at the table by the window, cracking his knuckles one by one, as his eyes gradually dimmed and slid out of focus. But then the ancient dice game played with knuckle-bones appeared before him, and he looked down at his hands. A foolish habit, a wastrel habit. The poor old bones were being worn away on their own quickly enough. Look at all those spots on his skin, like drops of wax spattered on old weathered parchment. Parchment, Pergamum, poor lost Troy; everything would crumble. Panic rattled gently in Oswaldo's chest, and he crossed his arms, shivering. Shutting his eyes, he saw it all, that dark, hollow cavern inside him that waited, inside his skull, within his frail ribs, until they crumbled away. And what then? And what then? He could not comprehend this blackness; he would not condone it.

He opened his eyes and stood up quickly, the chair clattering upon the terrazzo floor. The clean, sharp sound was reassuring. You are graceless, he thought. Indulging in rumination and introspection of the most evil sort. You fancy that you are alone in this predicament? Go out! he ordered himself. Look out! He hurried to the window and opened his eyes and mouth wide to the air, to the sky.

Lucinde was coming: what could be better? His dear friend, the young woman he'd privately imagined as his daughter, his niece, ever since she first turned up with a grant. At once the world before him was full of color and hope. She'd be here tomorrow, and in fact what he would do now, before lunch, was go to the Rialto market for flowers.

Lucinde's cab traveled the same route as Max's but in the opposite direction, flying past the shacks and abandoned gas stations along the plundered, poisoned road to the airport. She had felt vague and distant ever since he called. That he had actually come here—a strange dream. Yet she barely dreamt. No more than she had lines on her palms.

She looked at her hands lying neatly in her lap. They were smooth and white, and her arms were white, too, long and a little plump: arms from another century, unblemished. The cab barreled on, past rental storage units, kudzu and sumac and trash. It was all somehow dangerous, now that he was there. As the cab turned onto the highway, she checked her plane tickets. New Orleans to New York; New York to Venice. How lucky that it was already planned, and that Oswaldo was so kind, and that there was the added cause of bringing some comfort to Vera. Otherwise it would be too clear that she was simply fleeing.

From what?

Kudzu was everywhere! Clasping, creeping. Lucinde could nearly hear it. She rolled up the window, the image through the pane sliding a little with the glass.

Max realized, as he showered in the lopsided bathroom, that during that whole week the previous fall he had never once seen Lucinde's house. He had never really pictured her living in a house, as if she had simply appeared from the air of the city itself. With a towel wrapped around his waist, he dripped across the blue carpet and took from his briefcase one of her letters, if you could call it that, a blissful scribble on a piece of something that wasn't exactly paper. On the back of the envelope, whose stamps proved that it was real and had indeed passed through mechanical life, was her flamboyantly printed address. Yes, he thought as he stood there a moment blinking his watery eyes, he would do it. Even making the decision, he felt a butterfly of danger.

The walls of his hotel room were painted an intense peacock blue, and the furniture was animate, turbaned, and ringed, the upholstery brocaded, all of it with a smell that Max thought almost had dimension as he opened the creaking armoire, a smell that came closer to being a color than any smell he had known. He dressed in a wrinkled salmon shirt, dun trousers, and woven sandals from Spain, with which he must, sadly, wear socks. Standing in front of the mirror, he pulled the shirt right, saw that he'd misbuttoned it, rebuttoned it, and vigorously rubbed his scalp, trying to organize the little coils. Outside the window was a shaggy palm trunk, the torn tips of a banana plant, and a remnant of floating moss; looking at them, he thought, Safari!

On the streetcar Max took a seat behind a small black girl whose braided hair was held by twenty-eight bright plastic baubles, fuchsia, purple, lime. He noticed his knee bouncing as the tram rattled downtown and latched his hands tightly around it. A few blocks down Saint Charles several pale tourists boarded, along with an ancient black man wearing a straw hat, while outside, a young woman with red hair stood staring at him, positively staring, her arms tightly crossed; he looked away and folded his own arms reflexively. Once the streetcar had moved on, he opened the window and put his head out to the blowing air, mouth open.

The city passed in layers, first the deep greens of the trees and the white or yellow wood houses, then a sudden harsh glare of concrete, a brief murkiness as the tracks ran beneath the highway, then the glassy, shadowy zone downtown. Max got off at the last stop, on the edge of the Quarter. In the bright sun he put a hand to his collar and helplessly thought the word *redneck*. He approached the busy stickiness of the Quarter, with its tourists and buskers and shops, but at the last moment swerved away, instead climbing up the levee. There he felt like a sea captain as he shaded his eyes and watched a ferry struggle to cross the Mississippi; it was swiveling, midstream, against the current. He climbed back down the levee and went through the jammed market, where he thought sadly of the lost *pain patate*. Oh, the foods that were once so loved and then their recipes forgotten! Just think, the ingredients were all still to be had, only the few mag-

ical words were missing, but without them the whole creation
was lost. Yet it was sadder still when the things themselves disappeared. All the lost creatures bred out of existence, the brave
little muscled pigs that once ran through German woods . . . He
could not bear to think of such things, all the wonderful creatures and creations that were lost. They should not be allowed to
disappear like that. He would have one of his new assistants research *pain patate* right away, he decided, and then, as soon as he
had found a place, he himself would prepare it. Cheered at once
with the resolution, Max proceeded to Esplanade.

Esplanade, Rue Royale. He counted the houses, tapping index
finger to thumb, and before he was ready, he was there, on the
sidewalk right in front of her house. He hurried across the street
so as not to be too close and placed his back safely against an
iron fence, his body partly hidden by an explosion of peeling
trunk and camouflaging pink blossoms, around which he could
peer.

A temple, yes. You would really have to say it was a sort of
miniature temple. A raised cottage, with a yellow cornice and
several white columns, topaz shutters behind them, all of it six
steps above ground among a flounce of palmettos. Max squinted
as several cars and a bus barreled by, their exhausts blowing his
hair back, and he was so satisfied with what he had found that his
stockinged toes twitched with delight.

The house was shuttered, but it was no trouble at all for Max
to see through those white walls to the tinkling fountain inside,
the turbaned eunuchs fanning his odalisque with palmetto
fronds. And now it seemed that she was not just an odalisque but
a *shabby* odalisque—perfect! How perfect that the house's walls
were cheap brick, only plastered and painted to look like ma-
sonry, and that they were cracked, and that the steps emerging
from the spiky greenery were chipped at the edges, crumbling.

Perfect that the house was so much less perfect than he'd feared: besiegeable that way. And further perfect that the shutters were latched and that a fine layer of pollen clung to the steps, as that meant she truly wasn't home, she hadn't lied to him, she had gone away.

Josephine walked to the office slowly and with great care, because it was day twenty-eight and she was actually still holding. About which she was trying hard not to think, never before in her disorganized life having made it past day twenty-four.

Palm trees, banana plants, camellias, jasmine, rose, bougainvillaea, fig. She concentrated first on the plant names and then on the street names, to see, as she had nearly each day since arriving in New Orleans last year, if there was any system at all in their sequence; she concentrated on the sidewalk as well, because it often needed negotiating. Huge live oaks grew along Saint Charles, their roots splitting and buckling the sidewalk pavement, so that she had to step up or down sometimes more than a foot or cautiously keep her balance on slabs that wobbled and cantilevered up. Antonine Street. Nine or so blocks to go, then safe.

She'd been telling herself for the past three days that of course it couldn't be true.

Could it?

Positive thoughts, Doctor Gare had said.

Positive, yes, but as everyone said, don't want it too much: too much pressure.

Josephine looked around hopefully. Dusty leaves, crooked branches, a wadded Kleenex in the grass.

Positive thoughts. Positive! Positive.

Yet it was such a thin, flat word, she couldn't help but think. Whereas *negative* had a greenish phosphorescence, much more intriguing.

What were thoughts, then, chemical? Could they fan through you like poison?

She really should think about something else. For instance, what she had to do today: start working on a proposal about the Mississippi, shrimp being poisoned, dead fish. A new Mississippi Research Center, that's what was wanted, and she, in her office that had no windows but a steady glow from the computer, was to imagine this thing into being. And not just that but work out how to describe it, and to whom, so that money would come pouring in and the center would come to life. This was what she did: divined ways to make people give their money away. It was a job Josephine had lucked upon when they first arrived, and she found it so strangely easy that she looked down at her own hands, astonished. She did not meet these patrons herself—she could not possibly do that and mercifully didn't need to—just listened intently to the reports of the real fundraisers who put on their bright dresses and sallied forth to charm the old donors at Commander's for lunch. Then somehow, and truly it seemed divination, as Josephine sat at the glossy conference table with her back straight and her hair pinned up and listened attentively to the accounts of these lunches, the stray remarks the old millionaires had made or what they had ordered to eat, she knew exactly what to write to make the likes of old Claude Fontane take out his gold pen and pay for half a stadium or make Rose Cheri call up a few friends and establish a new visiting chair. You did it . . . he loves it . . . you've got golden fingers! the director had cried after only a month, collapsing with her brooch and pumps in a chair. As Anton said, Look at you—you're gold.

Gold.

Constantinople Street, Marengo, Milan, although here she now knew they said *My*-lan. From which real city, Milano itself, Anton was four hours by train. He hadn't called this morning, and that was a relief, although it was true she had hurried from the apartment early so that he'd miss her if he tried. Because she didn't know what they would say if they spoke. They were both holding their breaths.

She wondered if it was actually possible.

But why not?

Why *not*?

It just didn't seem possible, that was all. Some sense she had, some unclear sense she'd always had, of a slippery dark foulness inside.

Do not think.

So, a Mississippi Research Center. She would think about the Mississippi. She must learn its length and various depths and just what swam within it, and this she could hardly wait to do, picturing the silence, the darkness, sturgeon nosing along. She must learn what else flowed secretly into the waters from all that machinery upriver, plumes of poison floating downstream. And on top of that she must learn about dikes and levees and waterworks and pumps, just how far underwater the whole city was likely, one day, to go. Peaceful days in the library, then, and interviews with engineers and biologists, and thoughtful thumbings through charts and maps. The water itself was undrinkable, everyone told her that. So she dutifully filled up gallon jugs at the machine outside the grocery store for a quarter apiece and lugged them back home. Cancer Corridor, this stretch of river was called; Josephine imagined it rushing through pipes and out taps, seeping in through pores in the shower, and wondered how many showers equaled drinking a gallon.

Napoleon Avenue. She waited to cross, picturing Napoleon himself standing there stalwart amid the cars and the hazy exhaust. There was a Josephine Street too, down beyond the Garden District. It was near the numbered streets. And if the numbers extended logically, it would be Negative Second.

Don't think.

Immaculate was what she'd been thinking up on Doctor Gare's table. What with the glass and the light and the crisp paper robe and Doctor Gare's soft white fingers.

Immaculate. Which Anton really *was*! His transparent skin, his clear, clean bones, his strange, awkward, innocent height. Determination burned right through him! She could see it, sometimes, in his cheeks, the skin on the high bones radiant. But squinting at him, she could also see what he wished so hard to hide, how just inside that fine skin was a sea of inexplicable mortification, and every little thing he did was a desperate fight to subdue it.

A streetcar was blocked by a car idling on the tracks beside her, the conductor irritably ringing his bell. A convertible had been in the same place yesterday; a sunglassed young woman in the passenger seat had held a champagne glass in her hand, lifted it, drained it, and tossed it onto the street, its breaking clear and light. Champagne, champagne, that *g* like a bubble, popping silently against the roof of the mouth. Josephine could nearly taste it.

Sometimes her tongue used to stay black with the wine that had seeped into it even a whole day later. Wine dark, wine sea, *epi oinopa ponton*.

But it was long ago, very long, since she'd done that sort of thing. Really, not since Anton.

The car moved on, the streetcar jolted to a start, and Josephine blinked, finding herself staring at two water-blue eyes that looked back at her, embarrassed, from the other side of the window. She turned away quickly and walked on as the tram rattled off in the other direction.

Josephine, Anton sometimes said, you know you'll have to do something someday.

What? She'd always laugh weakly, hearing this, while something spiraled inside her.

He would laugh, too, and take her hands. I mean, Josephine, you have to do something. Right now—you know—you're idling.

But look at my wonderful job!

I know, I know, but it's not good enough, it isn't really *you*. You're just killing time there, and you know it; it's just a distraction, something to do. One day you'll have to make something of all that gold in there. The languages! Why not? They offered you everything, fellowships for years!

Oh, but I only studied that for fun, she'd say, shrugging away, embarrassed.

And not the entomology either? Even though *they* said—

No, no, really, no, I couldn't, she'd say, laughing again.

But why?

Why?

Just can't, just can't. Can't say. It's just—

What?

Green light. Don't think. Just walk, hold on, don't hope, but be positive. Somewhere between hoping and positive.

Soniat Street, Dufossat, Valmont. A white Cadillac passed slowly by, the driver turning to look at her. To the right a small dog burrowed in a hedge.

Oh, but a baby . . .

It just didn't seem likely.

Why not?

Certainly this was closer than they'd ever been before.

What if everything was actually fine?

Could it be?

Why *not*?

Now, for a moment, just a brief moment, squinting as she walked past the glorious gardens and white-columned mansions and trash strewn in the gutters, Josephine let herself really hope: everything clicking into place, sunny little limbs running over green grass, vivid, clean, ordinary life.

Did she feel something inside?

She reached Jefferson and waited for the light.

Twenty-eight days were twenty-eight days. She'd never gotten past twenty-four. And shouldn't that mean something?

All right, she thought. She shut her eyes. If it happens, I promise, I'll try—

The light turned green, and she crossed. A sign. A green light was surely a sign.

Then, somewhere between Eleanore and State, Josephine felt that tugging behind her eyes, that finger winding itself idly in her hopeful sinews and giving a little pull. She started to laugh, out loud, right there on the sidewalk, as she passed by the grand houses built a century before, over the roots that shattered the sidewalk like huge fish waking before plunging deep. Already she felt it inside her ribs. And then, unmistakable, there was the falling away, so that by the time she reached Audubon Park it had been perfected again, the failure, blood wet between her legs.

Lucinde had arrived in Oswaldo's house as she always did, like light or a wind, the doors all banging, her voice filling the palazzo's cold hallways. Oswaldo found his eyes wide open, found himself creeping down the warped stone steps and along the flaking walls, and he took refuge in his study, deeply pleased to be hosting this creature but much more secure alone. Already the phone had been ringing, and she strode up and down the terrazzo floors in her high heels, gesturing, making appointments. She knew everyone everywhere, people she'd worked with on sites or some such, people she'd contracted to make settings and props. Looking at Lucinde as she spoke on the phone and gestured, touching a hand now and then to her hair, he saw a bright figure in full stream, eddies all around her, while he himself, he thought as he turned to the window and gazed balefully out at the sea, had drifted to the river's end. All he did these days was shuffle about, write out his checks to the Fondazione.

But when he and Lucinde went out for the evening stroll, the *passeggiata*, her gloved hand light upon his arm, he thought, How long since I have had such a creature on my arm as I travel this familiar route? It was crowded that evening, the procession of modeled faces and coiffed hair and tailored wool and fur winding through the passages of his fabulous, sinking city. The sky had just grown dark, and the air was cool but complicated with the smells of tobacco, perfume, burnt sugar, and coffee. Heels clattered on the stones, soft loafers slid, voices murmured as faces were held for appraisal, boys darted after girls drifting by arm in arm, and people called out to each other from either side of the *calle* as the stream moved like a parade between window displays of books and prints and chocolates, cosmetics, rare maps, silk scarves, a jeweled lion. Lucinde had already been stopped twice by people at whom Oswaldo peered through eyes that felt old and distant and fogged. He had probably known most of those who passed, or at least their grandparents, uncles, aunts, but it seemed they kept coming, younger and new, and he could no longer keep track.

"Oswaldo! What is it?"

How to explain? It was foolish, not worthy. "I don't know," he said. "I want—" but he couldn't go on, he did not know what he wanted, and just then someone new greeted Lucinde, a pale woman with shadowed eyes and a fall of dark hair. Above the women's conversation, full of vehemence and firm pressings of hands, he let his eyes grow dim again.

"Oswaldo," said Lucinde after a time. She smiled. "Here's Vera."

He made an effort, frowned, shook her hand. All he could think, as he looked at the woman's prominent jaw and uneasy dark eyes, was *New World*. She blushed, and Lucinde pulled her closer to resume their conversation, Lucinde's opal eyes and this woman's intent on each other, unblinking. Again Oswaldo grew vague; he watched them, couldn't hear them, felt himself disappear.

Oh, he was ungrateful! Here was his dearest young friend, Lucinde, come to visit, here on his arm, a magnetic woman who streamed light as she moved. How could he want anything? He should not. At last she was released from her conversation, and she and Oswaldo moved slowly on, over the wooden bridge, past the Accademia gallery, and around the corner, the passage here narrow and resounding with voices. The art bookstore at the turn had windows full of Bellini prints, rose and lime and lavender and gold, and magazine covers of sleek new buildings. They paused, and as Oswaldo gazed in the window, he found his own reflection by mistake: the walrus moustache, the forlorn eyes. He glanced at Lucinde's mirrored eyes and found her nodding at someone, a tall dark-haired man with a bitter mouth.

"Drink?" said Oswaldo, pulling her away.

"So tell me what's wrong," she said as they went into a bar.

He frowned and shrugged, passed her a Campari. "Cin-cin," he said. He sipped and pondered her eyes, which seemed to change with the light. Since she had come and her merciless heels had clattered on his floors, he'd become more aware of the stone, the terrazzo, seen that the floors had grown as warped and waving as those of the church of San Marco.

"Do you find my house greatly aged?"

Lucinde laughed. "It's ancient."

He sighed. "Who was that young woman again?"

"Oswaldo. She's one of your own."

"Oh?" He felt dim again, so tired.

"She's here with a grant. Vera Ponto."

"Oh yes. Yes, yes. She's the one who does saints?" Lucinde nodded. "And who," he said, "was that last one?"

"In the window? The man? I can't quite remember. I think someone from home."

Oswaldo poked at the lime in his drink.

"Did I tell you," she went on, "that I've got someone waiting for me there?"

"Actually in your house?"

She shook her head slowly and propped an elbow on the bar. "Not as bad as that yet." She smiled. "A traveler. From far away."

"And he's sailed to New Orleans for you?"

"Yes, flown."

Afterward, as Oswaldo's boat raced over the water in the cold night air, Lucinde looked at the city and said, "Architect." She turned to Oswaldo with satisfaction. "Something to do with water building."

"What?"

"The man in the window. Anton? Stiers."

Lach strolled up the Schiavone embankment to San Marco, cut in, and walked happily among the smoke and clattering heels and voices toward the Accademia. One arm swung while the other held a cigarette the way he always held cigarettes when he was here, his elbow bent and hand resting companionably at his stomach.

It had taken several trips across the lagoon to ferry all his and Francesca's things from the little pink house on the Giudecca to her place by San Zaccaria, but Lach had done it himself, valiant, while Francesca sailed on ahead. He was being very good to let Vera stay in the house, but then again, he told himself, what he was doing to her was just atrocious. Goodbye, house, he had said sadly as he turned the key in the lock the last time and gave the door a friendly pat. Don't forget me. It will only be a few months. He passed it every day on his way to the studio on the Giudecca and looked solicitously up at the windows—sad little thing, all alone.

He loved the *passeggiata*! The smoke and perfume, the singsong exchanges; he could just lean against a wall and watch the parade forever. He tramped up the wooden steps of the bridge and gazed at the famous view, first one way, then the other, took a deep breath, and shook his lank hair from his eyes.

But suddenly he was disconcerted. That woman, just a few steps before him. He knew her. Floating down the wooden steps, pausing now and then to gesture, was that friend of Vera's, the one from New Orleans he'd never liked, with those cold, laughing eyes and lazy big white legs. She was wearing a terrible green hat. Usually no one he knew was in Venice in winter, and now not only was Vera at large, but here too was that awful Miss New Orleans. Lach could not help but feel besieged. He hesitated a moment, then bounded past her, around the gallery, over the first bridge, and into the bookstore at the turn, gasping. He should really stop smoking. Tomorrow!

So had Vera summoned her, for fortification? He had always hated how those two talked, those cold eyes going up and down him. In the bookstore he stared at an image of something on a cover and picked up one of the magazines. Then, only a minute later, when he happened to glance up, there she was, actually gazing in the bookstore window. And whom did she have at her side but Oswaldo Manin? Not just at her side; both her gloved hands were wrapped about his arm.

Lach didn't move until they had gone on, concentrating hard on the magazine, and then he threw it down and rushed from the shop and set off in the opposite direction, away from the heels and perfume and voices of the crowd and across Dorsoduro to the Zattere embankment. It was quiet there and dark; his chest hurt. Wind blew at his coat and his hair, water sloshing against the *fondamenta*. All he wanted was to get on a boat and go over to his peaceful little pink house and work, head down, until everyone was gone.

But of course he couldn't, could he? He stopped abruptly, lit a cigarette, then turned around to walk not up the embankment but down it, toward the Salute instead. A few steps more, and his house came into view across the choppy lagoon, looking so sweet beside the glowing Redentore church, its two little windows dark. Well, maybe Miss New Orleans had come on her own. But no doubt she knew Vera was here. No doubt they'd seen each other. Maybe she was even staying at his house! He could picture Vera with her, see the sympathetic, disdainful pale eyes as Vera told her everything. Yes, her face would be intent upon all the nasty details. Oh, but there would be lots of that; he could imagine the faces of all Vera's friends, earnest over coffee, over tea, and how she would run her hands through her black hair and chew her soft, blood-filled lips.

But I'm letting you stay in the house, he thought, even though it was the main reason I came! Lach nearly stamped his foot. He stared over the lagoon at the Redentore, tried to remember something famous about its proportions, couldn't, but remembered at least the plague that had caused it to be built and something he'd once read about how much Ruskin hated Palladio. Poor Palladio. Stories like that always made Lach sad, stories about artists long since turned back into mud before anyone even appreciated them. Terrible! Behind the glowing church the sky blew blustery, dark, and the light reminded him of something, the color. He tapped at his cigarette, watched the ash fall, took another deep drag, then checked up and down the bank quickly before tossing the cigarette into the water. What was it about that color? He could just barely see what he was trying to remember . . . Vera's skies, he realized. Her skies were darker than the grounds, midnight skies, nearly every blue with just a little titanium, so that the picture would be just as heavy on top as on bottom, she said. And why not? he remembered thinking, shrugging. Of course it should work upside down, too. She made the paint very thick.

"Pavonazzo," he had once said as he stood before a piece she was working on. She hadn't heard at first, absorbed, and he realized that his eyes were tearing. This was just last summer—who would think!—just after he'd found the house, just after he'd found Francesca. When already those wicked traveling wings were flapping about his feet.

"What?"

"Pavonazzo," he repeated, his voice breaking a little. "A color once worn in Venice for mourning."

And he'd turned quickly away, but he knew she'd noticed his tearing eyes because he saw the look in her own, that first little flash of alarm. Did she know he was mourning already, because he would have to leave her?

Oh, Vera, he thought, I'm sorry. He sighed into the wind. Maybe it was just as well that Miss New Orleans had come. She would be sure to give Vera some comfort.

Humming then, Lach walked home.

Anton was supposed to meet Robert at the bookstore at six-thirty and had already spent twenty minutes inside and then another ten minutes out front, in case Robert somehow hadn't seen him, when that woman smiled at him and nodded. Of course he'd nodded back, but he'd felt himself flush. He just could not think who she was. An imposing woman, heroic even, somehow of another era—her gloves or the shape of her face. He knew he knew her, but it could be from anywhere, anytime in the past few years. Not Providence. Or New York. Savannah, maybe? Charleston? It was in a room, he could nearly see it, a large room. . . . Of course, he realized suddenly, New Orleans, an opening at the arts center. Venice was so electric, all sorts of people turned up here, little contacts. You might see anyone. He had to keep his eyes open.

He shifted his position and focused again on the architecture books in the window. Titanium cladding. Was that actually titanium? And some kind of treated glass. The reflection made him seem to be inside the window, on display, intent eyes, that slightly off-kilter furrow; his mouth looked tense, injured, so he moved it around to relax it. Surreptitiously he looked at his watch. Thirty-five minutes late! In a spasm Anton stepped away from his mooring and at once was caught up in the current of people and carried all the way to the next square and nearly over the next bridge; with an effort he broke free, crossed over the *calle*, and joined the flow coming back. He detached himself once more and resumed his post by the window. Not just titanium but lots of glass that looked as if it had water inside it.

When Josephine called him yesterday, he could tell at once that it hadn't worked. He absorbed the information silently, felt it slide fine and sharp between his ribs. But it rarely worked the first time, Doctor Gare himself had said. No reason not to keep trying.

So what comes next? Anton had asked her; in the background he could hear birds. We're up to shots now, she said, because the pills won't work anymore. Shots! he cried. Really? Then wait until I'm back. You certainly can't do that alone. But she'd said no, the timing was better now. Because what about the insurance?

Well, that was true. And whose fault was it? His. A man without stability, a clam, clinging to rocks, leaving dreamy Josephine to do everything herself. Shots!

Anton drew a little syringe with his finger on the window and then wiped it away, embarrassed. He pictured her, half asleep in the green New Orleans light, fumbling with the needles and vials, sitting on the edge of the tub, looking down at her stomach. Then she'd take the needle, and he could see her plunge it in wrong; he never even liked to see her with knives. Accident-prone, heedless, careless, and still she'd look up laughing from her crumpled, pale, bruised legs. The ghost of his erased syringe returned on the glass with his hot breath; it looked more like a campanile, like the tower of San Giorgio. Saint George and the dragon: the spear slipping into the beast's throat, blood spurting upon the rotting limbs of all the fallen heroes. Anton wiped it away again with his sleeve.

Last year, when she'd had one of the tests to see what was

wrong, her lifted legs glowed in the dark room as the ink was injected inside her, and on the screen he saw the ink slowly fill her womb and meander out to either side. He'd looked at her, amazed, but she was lying with her arm draped over her eyes as if she had fallen asleep. She would work so hard at a project, intent and utterly absorbed, and when it was done, she'd waver a moment and then just fall asleep. As if without a given task she had nowhere to go and sank. But all the things she could do if she tried, all the little brilliances! Sometimes it seemed that she had let herself fall into that job, or fall into his hands, just to be relieved of herself. For three years now she had figured in his photographs of sea buildings and bridges and ferries, just her fleeting shadow, her silhouette, or one blurred leg as she walked away.

Wake up, Josephine! It's time to wake up.

"Antonio!"

He spun around, reconstructed his face at once. "Roberto!"

Then they walked away, two men striding in the river of people, and went to a bar for a drink.

It took Max weeks to find the right apartment. He was driven around by a realtor friend of the department secretary's, a sparrowlike woman named Clare who drove her car fast over the crumbling roads with the air-conditioning blasting. They inspected a warehouse loft with new thin brown carpet, which made Max sneeze explosively; they passed quickly through slaves' quarters with a peeling wooden balcony and a trapdoor in the ceiling; they drove slowly by but did not visit a white brick bungalow in Metairie; a block up from Tchoupitoulas Street they considered a shotgun from which the tenant was being evicted, where clothes had been angrily strewn on the floor and an actual shotgun left on the bedside table; without a word Clare plucked a sock from the floor and dropped it over the gun. After that they saw a camelback and a much too expensive raised cottage. Finally they went to see an old ballroom for rent in the Quarter.

"It's trash," Clare said. "Infested with termites." But Max couldn't resist looking.

An iron gate on the street opened to a slot between two buildings, at the end of which was a small courtyard with mossy bricks, a lackluster fountain, banana plants, a hibiscus, a palm. External wooden stairs, perhaps a little unsteady and missing several planks, led to an internal gangway, whose condition Clare eyed skeptically and which in turn led to a door that didn't hang plumb. The door opened to a long ballroom full of dusty light. A chandelier hung from a crust of stucco in the ceiling, a pair of mirrored columns stood halfway down the room, near a fireplace with a marble mantel and several old chairs without seat bottoms, and the wooden floor sloped toward the street, spilling onto the balcony. At the near end was a kitchen like a ship's, thought Max, and an internal bathroom with no light. He went in, shut the door, his eyes wide and excited, fumbling in the darkness as the ghost of the bright ballroom hung before his eyes. When he came out, Clare was smoking and shaking her head, and Max said he would take it.

On the first of December he moved in, his Spanish sandals clattering happily over the floor in the large, light, echoing room. Nothing like London, nothing at all, bare and bright! The bed would face the fireplace, and imagine needing a fireplace here; even in December, two trips with heavy bags through the slot, into the courtyard, and up the rickety stairs had brought a damp glow to his face. Max felt extremely alive. He nearly kicked his heels in the middle of the long room. To have emerged from that rainy underworld! He could still feel its cold nets on his skin.

Nets. He stepped out the window to the balcony and looked down onto the street, both directions, then at the wrought-iron corncob fence across the way. Built, Clare had told him, by someone in the last century for his homesick Midwestern wife.

To comfort her?

To fence her in!

Max leaned on the railing and looked up at the hazy blue sky, then down Royale toward Esplanade. He could not quite see Lucinde's house but felt it there, as if light or warmth or some drawing scent emanated from it.

Let my beloved come into his garden and eat his pleasant fruits!

Suddenly he decided what he would do as soon as she got back: have a banquet. A spectacular feast to inaugurate the ballroom. And it would not just be for her, of course, but for lots of guests; he would dredge them up somehow, so that amid all the hubbub she would not notice the nets.

Up on the second floor of the old yellow house, live oak leaves were stirring at the window, but Josephine was gliding very deep, perhaps as much as sixty feet, in the bottommost channels of the Mississippi. Wake up, wake up; she knew she had to. Without opening her eyes, she knew it was the day.

But can you do it? Anton had asked her.

What, the injections? Sure. Why not?

The next step, Doctor Gare had proclaimed, rolling around on his stool and spreading out charts like cards. He had told her just how to do it.

Josephine would do it first thing, before she could even think. She got out of bed and went down the sunny hall, the cat trotting beside her. At the bathroom sink she washed her mouth, spewing the water out like a stone fountain. Here was the very expensive white box; in a litter of syringes lay the tiny bottle; and inside the bottle was the liquid, which she must inject inside her. There was an old woman who swallowed a spider. Swallowed a spider? She unfolded the instructions and placed them by the sink, a puddle soaking through. She took a syringe, unsheathed the needle, poked it through the rubber top of the bottle, and slowly drew up the liquid. Holding the syringe to the light, she pressed until a drop rose to the tip. She went to the edge of the tub and sat. Pinching a tuck of skin near her navel, she tapped it to numb it as Doctor Gare had shown her, then positioned the needle very close and readied her fingers to jab.

Alcohol! She had forgotten it, imagine. Leaving the syringe balancing on the edge of the tub, she went to the cabinet and took out the bottle. For a moment she held it open beneath her breathing mouth, the vapors flowing into the chambers of her head, the dreamy land of moths. She shut her mouth resolutely and went back to the tub. Then she pinched again at her stomach, swabbed it with the icy cotton, and held the point of the needle close.

It was a small needle, very fine, the metal shining in the sun.

She was supposed to poke it in at an angle. Suddenly she could not remember which.

Of course no one likes to do this, Doctor Gare had said.

Josephine held the needle at sixty degrees, then slanted it down to forty-five, then back up to sixty. Sixty looked better. It looked more convincing. She swabbed again for good measure, squinted her eyes, ignored the roaring, and stabbed. A line of blood came squirting out. She stared at it, astounded, and quickly withdrew the needle.

More alcohol! She tamped with cotton balls until the blood seemed to have stopped.

Well. That certainly wasn't right. She realized she was shaking a little. And now she'd have to start somewhere else. Although—she held the needle and syringe to the light—the liquid was still in there; that was a relief; otherwise it would have wasted almost a hundred dollars.

So maybe it was forty-five degrees? She picked a fresh spot on the other side of her stomach, swabbed it, pinched it, assured her grip on the syringe, and positioned the needle again. But she was sure there was something she'd forgotten. The little tuck of skin between her thumb and finger began to grow mottled. She tried again to remember, couldn't, so again ignored the roaring and plunged the needle in. Then suddenly she remembered: she was supposed to withdraw a little with the syringe to make sure she had not hit a vein. But there did not seem to be enough fingers, and the needle dangled from her stomach while with her thumb she tried to retract. Nothing at all came out, no blood; it wasn't clear what else could be inside her. Air?

The telephone rang, her fingers slipped, and the needle slid out and ran across her skin, scratching a line of fresh blood. She rested her hot forehead on the tiled wall. Miles and fathoms of water to Anton, and not just water, but hours.

It had been only thirty-five days since he'd gone, but already she had started to feel it, a slight shifting, a slipping. Even though she was being so good, even though she was working so hard. In fact she had been staying even longer at work than usual, much longer, deep among her papers and charts and diagrams of pumps and levees, and what with the days getting shorter, it was dark when she'd finally walk alone across the green, dark as she'd ride the streetcar home, dark in the apartment, as well, so there was nothing to do but go to bed early, and that meant she could get to work early, too.

Seven rings, eight rings, nine, ten. Then it was quiet, the ghost of the last ring dissolving in the walls.

At least two weeks of these shots, Doctor Gare said, and then the others as well. You must be completely suppressed, he said, before we induce the eggs.

Josephine looked down again at her scratched, mottled stomach, then out the window toward Mrs. Mouton's garden, her roses, crepe myrtle, sweet olive, and palms. The lady herself stood on the steps in a bathrobe, her hair pale blue against the paler blue house. Out in the private early sun, she slipped her hand comfortingly into the top of her robe.

Josephine looked at the needle.

There was an old woman who swallowed a spider.

Many spiders, she happened to know, inseminated their mates with extra legs like syringes. Whereas male bedbugs drilled through the female's shell.

An anole ran up the window frame, froze when it saw her see it, and turned slowly from green to brown, all the way from its tiny alligator nose to its slender pointed tail. They could release their tails to predators, she knew, as stick insects could give up a leg and flee. And female stick insects produced a dozen eggs a day and flung them away with a flick; oysters spewed millions right into the sea.

Tiny, pearly things: out they tumbled each month, between her legs, then through the drains, under the streets, into the Mississippi and the Gulf and the shining wide sea. That red baby Anton had drawn on her stomach had washed down the drain and could be out there even now, tangled up in the sargasso weeds like trash.

Just how suppressed is completely suppressed?

One night, before Anton, she'd emerged from the black to find herself in a bathroom mirror somewhere, no idea where her clothes were.

Why did you always do such things? Anton sometimes asked, his blue-veined white hands on her shoulders.

Again she tightened her fingers on the syringe and pinched a patch of skin. She swabbed it, tapped it, bit her teeth together, jabbed the needle in, and injected.

Lach was careful to stay away from his house, only looking at it sadly from the vaporetto as he journeyed between Francesca's dark apartment near San Zaccaria and his studio in the boathouse on the Giudecca. Although he hadn't seen Vera, he knew she was there because one evening he noticed, with a terrible clutch in his stomach, his own two front windows lit. But he hadn't called or gone over, because surely that was best. Wasn't it? Not too heartless, too unconcerned? He wasn't altogether certain and picked the phone up once or twice and pondered, knitting his brows, but then put the receiver down again. He'd been in this sort of situation before, after all, he was embarrassed to remind himself. There was always so much *temptation*, so much falling back; it only ever made things worse. Bad enough she was actually here.

He was painting today, at Francesca's, a freezing day that would have made the Giudecca studio far too cold, although Francesca's place was not much better. The floor was made of tiles like a church, old and scratched and worn. A thin, chilled light fell through the tall windows. Lach had to wear two pairs of socks and two sweaters over his sailor-striped shirt, as well as a scarf wound twice about his neck, and he cupped his cigarette with stiff fingers for warmth. The show would be in—what, two months?

He shivered, paced back and forth over the tiles, and swung his arms in a few arcs to warm up. When he redid the pink house, he would absolutely unseal the fireplace, and it cheered him even now to think of sitting in front of a big fire with a drink, under some nice Irish blankets with Francesca. He turned back to his canvas. The colors seemed to have changed. He went to another corner of the room to look at it from there, but it was just as bad. Sighing, he lit another cigarette, went to the window, and gazed down at the *campo*. The antiques store had put a lop-sided ancient stool out front, with some sort of wheel leaning against it. A boy was kicking a red ball by himself, thudding it into the wall by the church; a couple huddled arguing over a map; a woman emerged from the narrow passageway, a woman in a funny hat. He looked more closely, then stepped quickly back. So she was still here, Miss New Orleans. He watched as she crossed the *campo* to the church.

What was she doing here anyway? She found film sites or something in New Orleans now; she organized events. After a minute he returned to the window to stub his cigarette against the outside wall, a shower of sparks falling down the façade. Then he realized with horror that she was still there, waiting on the church steps for the doors to be opened, and as he looked at her, she looked right at him. He stumbled back into the room and stared at his feet on the tiles.

She had *always* made him nervous! For one thing, she was big. Although often he liked big women, he'd liked lots of big women. Her bigness was different, though, softer but more dangerous, big like a queen or an angel. There was something about her that was slightly loathsome, or not loathsome, that was too strong, but *repellent*. She was too smooth, impenetrable, like wax or soft ivory, and if you cut her, she'd be the same straight through, all white and smooth and always smiling. Technically she was attractive, sure—more than attractive, hypnotic; he'd seen men bump up against her and fall stunned. Yet she seemed to regard them with a sort of ecstatic contempt. She had always disliked him.

Lach went back to his painting and stood before it, his face crumpled and not with mirth. It was distracting that she was just across the *campo* in his church; distracting that she was in Venice at all! Together with Vera: it was like a shadow at the corner of his eye. God only knew what they were saying, or even *plotting*. I'm sorry, he thought. All right? I'm sorry! It's just that I can't help it. Things change.

He picked up a split tube of cadmium yellow. It was all beginning to seem ruined, that Dionysus leap from the loft in New York, that spring over the ocean to Venice. And he'd wanted to start everything new!

Lach stirred the can of thinner slowly with a brush, drawing an oily dark sludge from the bottom. Dregs, he thought. Sea bottom. Everything got ruined so *easily*. He peered into the can at the oiliness, black swirls, and streaks. But bits of light still glinted. Then all at once Venice and color and water and light slipped together kaleidoscopically in his mind, and he found himself bright again, his old happy self, with his crinkled, debauched eyes. Because none of that really mattered, did it? *This* was all that mattered: to be where he was, doing what he did, taking his modest little place in the long glorious line from Vivarini.

Finally the sacristan opened the doors, and Lucinde went in, passing from the chill, bright day into the smell of incense, the dark stillness, the air of cold age. As her eyes adjusted, she felt her way forward, her hip grazing a block of marble, her feet careful on the uneven tiles. Already she could see the painting she'd come for; it had been just before her eyes ever since she'd made her way up the narrow *calle*, its colors faint, remembered. It hung in the left aisle of the church, and even in the dimness she could see it, finer than everything around it, giving out a subtle glow. She stood before it a moment in the dark.

Then she dropped a coin in the box, and with a thunk and a flash the painting flared before her: sacred conversation, Virgin and saints, the figures so familiar, so dear. The young woman and child sat enthroned in the center, and around them stood the pensive saints, an angel at their feet. And the colors . . . the rose pleats, the soft far clouds, the ashy beard, the tarnished brocade, the heavy red book with fluttering pages, the finger holding the page in place.

Lucinde stood before the painting and gazed at the eyes of the figures. She gazed at them as intently, as privately, as she might gaze into her own reflected eyes. As if there were someone else actually there, and she might really be seen.

The figures gazed away, each one away, not even at each other, yet it seemed to her that something hung between them, a constellation drawn among all those thoughtful eyes. Sacred conversation, silent conversation. Just what are you speaking of? Lucinde wondered. She had always wondered this—in all the sacred conversations, but especially this one, where the conversation seemed so intent. It was not even a conversation, but silent, without words; it seemed more a belief that hovered about the figures, like the invisible music of the angel singing at their feet. What, then, do you believe? What does that angel sing?

Music of the angels, music of the spheres. Lucinde tried to imagine the spheres and their music: abstract and pure, their tone like that of a triangle, clear. She contented herself that the silent conversation was something like this, a music that was pure concord, a concord that was surely love. And so a love that was invisible, a love that was intangible, but a love that was all the same known.

Anton was staying with his students in Venice today, concerned that they hadn't been impressed enough with all the marvelous works around them. As if they hadn't quite comprehended that the extraordinary city hadn't just arisen in one piece from the sea but had all been painstakingly *made*. He'd marched them to the Ca' d'Oro, and his gray-sleeved arms flew about as he called their attention to the palace's loggias, proportions, and tracery; as he explained the expenses to which rich old Marin had gone with Istrian stone, ultramarine, and gilding, all of it long since faded or carried away, leaving stone humbled but brilliant. Yet look how it floats! he cried to his students. See how the light bounces from the water upon the tracery, all of it rippling together, all the elements dissolving! From there he shepherded them to the church of the Gesuiti, where again his arms waved about as he pointed to the baroque ornamentation, the bleached sculptures, the interior hung with marble like damask. And from there they went to the little church of Santa Maria dei Miracoli, where once more Anton strode and grew hoarse as he rapped his knuckles upon the marble disks that had been sliced from porphyry columns and applied to the façade, and he drew diagrams in the air to elucidate how color tricked the eye. All the brilliance! he exclaimed. All the effort!

Finally he was exhausted, and when his students had trooped inside the church, dutifully peering up at the gilded coffers in the ceiling, he paid the grinning sacristan and slumped into a pew, gazing dully at the altar. He'd had another evening with Robert last night at Paradiso Perduto, and afterward, in his dreams, he'd wandered through meandering, shining passages that smelled of urine and cat; otherwise there were spears and needles and Saint Georges, and he would never drink grappa with Robert again. No, not Robert, *Roberto*. Who had just won a huge competition, he told Anton with his peaceful gray eyes as he lifted a finger for another round. He had shown up, more or less, for Anton's crits and had given a passable lecture, but otherwise he'd produced no help at all. Although he said, *Di' mi, Antonio*, what are you looking for? To which Anton laughed and flung out his hands. Isn't it obvious? he cried. Possibilities! Something permanent! At that Roberto lowered his lids. Ah, permanence, he had said sagely. I wonder what that really is.

Stone, thought Anton now. A job!

He became aware again of his students milling about, of the fussy sacristan, the cold, waxy smell, the carved forms decorating the altar. On one side knelt a stone angel, sending his silent message across the steps to the bewildered young stone girl. *Miracoli*, annunciation.

So is it all right, the shots? he'd asked Josephine six days ago, and since then she hadn't answered the phone. He'd been lying in bed, one hand on his chest, startled a little at the feel of his own skin. Are you doing the injections all right? But she only laughed, and he could nearly see her throat, see that green vein, her thin teeth. Of course I am, she said, it's nothing. Nothing? he said. Really? Well . . . Again she'd laughed. Maybe just a few mistakes.

Anton squirmed in the pew, coughed, took out his black

book, and went up the steps of the altar to join his students
drawing the carvings. Stone mermaids with little horse forelegs,
bearing small boys upon their backs; he wanted to touch the polished stomachs each time he saw them, comforting. Slender stone
stomachs, delicate hands; he did not like to think about Josephine jabbing with needles. He'd found her once at the kitchen
sink watching with interest as drops of blood rolled down her
hand. His pencil followed a mermaid's silhouette from waist to
cheek; her stone eyes stared at him, unseeing. He thought of
Josephine as he'd first seen her, that icy night in Providence. Or
not first seen her, for he already knew who she was: she'd just
won a prize as she'd so often won prizes, thinking nothing of
them, her picture in the university paper. He had been hurrying
up the hill after giving his lecture, slide carousels in his arms, the
frigid air cutting into his lungs, when he heard a pattering of feet
behind him and quick, sobbing breaths. He turned just at the
moment she ran under a streetlight. But she saw him, too, and
stopped. And for a moment they stood there, she in the yellow
light, he in the shadows, and then he saw that she was barefoot,
her feet bleeding on the broken ice. He didn't know what to do,
but suddenly—with her wild red hair, her bloody feet—she
seemed an apparition that would vanish, leaving him like a wan-
derer clasping nothing in the woods. He coughed to break the
spell and asked if anything was wrong. She blinked and seemed
to wake a little. Why, no, she said, what makes you say so? He
couldn't answer, so asked what he could do. Well, I guess home,
she said, with a sleepy smile. But she couldn't say where home
was, so after roaming the streets in a cab, he gave up and took her
to the extravagant place he'd sublet for his stay. There she went
directly upstairs, climbed into the postered bed, and curled up,
weeping softly like a child. He watched from the door until she
grew quiet, looking at her shuddering form as if she were a ru-

ined, bloodied mermaid. At last he went back down and slept on the sofa, or tried to sleep, seeing through the darkness this thin creature; at last, in his dreams her red hair had grown and crept down the creaking stairs, curling about him like flames.

It was awful when he told her the next day, for she remembered none of it. She'd shut her eyes, penitent, lost.

Anton stood up abruptly, hands and feet numb from the cold of the church despite the heat that suddenly ran through him. That had been three years ago tomorrow. He had nearly forgotten! He sent his students to lunch and ran from the church, and when he reached Rialto, bells were already ringing. He'd have flowers sent to her. Good luck! Good luck! We *will* do it this time! He pictured the flowers flying over the sea, petals scattering into the wind, onto the waves, and tumbling at last, heavy and fragrant, in through Josephine's window.

The tone of the banquet, Max decided, had to be just right. Festive and light and a little bit comic; otherwise Lucinde would be nervous. He'd been going through books for several days, both in the ballroom and in the office, which was a legitimate thing to do, given that he had to sort out the new chair's library and make all his requisitions.

There had to be a theme because that would dictate not only the menu but the decor and the dress, and everyone always felt safer that way. Furthermore, it would not be just an inauguration of his ballroom, but an inauguration of the new chair in the History of Food! The event would be completely safe, and also he'd have an invitation list. Max hurried from his cluttered office out to the department secretary. Elbows on the edge of her desk, he leaned forward and confided his plan and asked her to please help him draw up the list.

Good, then, that was settled. There would be guests, so there would be a banquet. Still, he needed the theme.

Sunday morning he was at home, the radio turned to the Cajun station as he sat amid boxes and books. His things had just come from Sea & Air, the Latin deliverymen straining through the slot between buildings and then one of them stoically stepping backward up the broken stairs. Max had unpacked only his books so far, looking at the other tea chests with unease, as if they bore foreign infection. He'd laid several old doors from one chest to the next to make a very long table, on which he now laid out books, lining them up not quite chronologically.

The theme could not be New Orleans or French or Caribbean or anything American at all, he decided. For a moment he pictured something ancient, but dismissed the possibilities with a taste of rancid oil in his mouth. Maybe something medieval. He was working, after all, on Subtleties at the moment, those elaborate, edible medieval constructions more like amusement parks than food. Marzipan architecture, cities of pastry and sugar, with elephants at the gates. Four and twenty blackbirds baked in a pie . . . Although of course they weren't really baked in it; what would be the point? No, the birds come out singing! He went through a book to remind himself of what might be involved, but soon he felt overwhelmed. Too much a sense of velvet and silk in these medieval things, and there was always the problem with proportions in the recipes: they weren't really recipes at all, just descriptions. Although he had done it once, a toil of love, baked such a marvelous pie. Here in fact was the recipe with a little secret joyous annotation he'd made in the margin, and the sight of it brought back to him full in the face the warmth of his London kitchen, Therese, her eyes as the butterflies had escaped from the crust. He closed the book, put it back in a box. From the radio a singer howled.

No, he did not want anything old. What he wanted was something *new*. Max stood up, twisted around, and touched his toes to shake away that old London cramp. He sat down again. There were still a few things like those ancient Subtleties today, after all, and he'd recently begun looking into them. Ice sculptures at banquets, for instance, and even tiered wedding cakes with little figurines on top, not to mention chocolate Easter bunnies and girls leaping out of cakes.

And in fact— Why not just call those Subtleties, too? Extraordinary he hadn't thought of it sooner! Max dug through a box until he found the book, with its strange green and pink and brown cover, which he'd once been sent to review. His banquet would be not just modern, but *future*. A Futurist Banquet. What more fitting than that?

Two weeks into the first set of shots and several days into the second, Josephine went again to Doctor Gare's office for her blood to be checked and then sat still as he studied her chart. By now her stomach was covered with swollen blue knots. She jabbed herself quickly, professionally, each morning, but these new shots were much worse than the others, like snakes in her veins, winding around her ribs, forcing her nerves to the surface. Her jaw or fist kept clenching, or else her hands would shake; at lunch once, inexplicably, she'd started to cry, but luckily she was alone in the office. Her mind altogether was becoming less orderly, no matter how she tried to control it; sharp little shards kept poking up. In the middle of an interview, as she'd been noting the heights and widths of the levees along the river and the lake, a flame of panic began to lick at her ribs, and despite how she tried to contain it, she found her cheeks burning and had to lower her head and scribble hard until it had subsided.

Doctor Gare rubbed his lips together and ran a finger down his chart; then he looked over it at her.

"Interesting," he said, his gaze going right through her skin to her blood. "You don't seem to be responding." His eyes lingered on her until her hair burned to the roots. "Usually one has responded more by now." He touched his chart with two white fingers, then touched the two white fingers together. "Why don't we just have a look?"

So up Josephine went under his shepherding hands, up onto the white-papered table, worried about her bare feet near his nose and her unshaven legs. She pressed her fingers to her eyes while he slid in the device and looked intently at his screen.

"No," he said, "I don't see much." He moved the instrument around inside her. "No, I can't say that I do."

After a time the thing came out of her body with a pop. "Up you get." Doctor Gare didn't quite look at his device but transported it with his gloved fingers to a counter, as she hurried into the dressing room and blotted the cold jelly between her legs.

"You'd better just carry on, though. Yes"—he waved a hand—"yes, carry on with the injections. You have," he added then, "been doing them? Not any problems, are there?"

No, of course not, she told him, not at all.

"Ah well," he said brightly. "There's still time."

So Josephine left with a prescription for another thousand dollars of vials and needles. The sidewalk on Prytania creaked as she stepped upon it, and a slab of concrete jutted up, exposing leathery roots in the darkness. Plastic beads hung from the branches of a tree; a pink crawfish shell lay in the gutter. The soil, she'd learned, was composed almost entirely of ground oystershell. Really, it belonged underwater. Most of the city was already six feet beneath sea level and sank another half inch each year.

She crossed Saint Charles to the K&B and gave the pharmacist the slip of paper, then walked up and down the aisles, looking at plastic Santas and candy and lotions and rows of tall dark bottles. One had fallen and broken and was being mopped up; she stood still in that aisle a moment. In New Orleans (a thin

black man with a moustache had told her as he'd packed her groceries) you can buy liquor twenty-four hours a day, seven days a
week, three hundred and sixty-five days a year. Thanksgiving and
Christmas, too. No cause at all ever to panic!

"Josephine Slayter?" said a voice over the intercom, and she
hurried back to the prescription counter, paid for her bag, and
left.

When she got home, a boy was knocking on the door, a tooth-
pick at the side of his mouth and a long, narrow box under one
arm.

Happy anniversary!

Three years.

When was he coming home?

Josephine went upstairs with the flowers and tried to remember that first night, which Anton had narrated so often she almost thought she could see it herself. It had been freezing, he
said, broken ice all over the streets. She remembered only the following morning, her eyes shut and the winter sun on her head so
hot that it seemed everything in her could finally burn away—
but then there he was, in the brightness, his dark hair, his
embarrassed eyes glancing shyly at her, his cheeks white and
flushing.

Upstairs in the kitchen she trimmed the stems, her hands
trembling until she fixed her eyes on them to make them stop.

Control yourself. You really should be able to do it.

She found a vase, a gift when they'd married, so soon after
that night on the ice, but Anton had wanted to start everything
at once; she could not believe it. She filled the vase with the
cloudy, undrinkable New Orleans water. *The water flowing in the*
Mississippi, she'd typed in her office, on the glowing green screen,
is like the blood in the veins of the nation, yet its condition by the time it
reaches New Orleans— Foul! But creatures did live in it, she now

knew. Carpsuckers, catfish, bowfin, bass. Even shovelnose sturgeon, which stayed near the bottom where the currents were slower, and the beautiful migrating eels. Female eels, with large pale eyes, which left the males waiting for years in the Gulf as they swam alone upriver, wriggling through niches in dams sometimes, even wriggling through muddy fields, wandering farther and farther. She looked at the bubbles tumbling into the jug. Not having any problems, are you? What, with the shots? She lowered the flowers into the water, but it didn't reach high enough, so she turned on the faucet again. Look at you, he'd said on the beach that first summer, the sand and sky dazzling behind him. You're gold.

Now the jug was overflowing. She poured out some water, wiped the bottom of the jug, took it to the dining room, and set it neatly in the center of the square white table. Anton's prints of ruins hung on two of the walls; in the third wall was a blocked-in fireplace. With her bare feet on his gold woolen rug, she suddenly sensed Anton himself in the room, the feel of his warm neck at her forehead, his large hands about her waist. She could close her eyes, lean against him, and simply disappear.

Josephine stood at the window, hand upon the sill, looking out at the dark, silent garden. It seemed so easy for those three years not to have happened at all, for her to be where she had been that night, wandering alone.

She hesitated a moment, rocking on her heels. It was nearly seven, so nearly two in the morning for him, late. She went to the bedroom and dialed anyway, winding the phone cord around her finger. Listening to the foreign rings, she pictured him, still as a bishop, his hand resting on his chest, while the rings circled out from the phone and lapped against his sleeping head.

Seven rings, eight rings, nine, ten.

At nearly two in the morning?

She hung up quietly and went back to the living room.

The cat blinked at her from the butterfly chair and very slowly yawned. The clock ticked over the mantelpiece; a few strands of Mardi Gras beads caught the light from the street, bright green, fuchsia, clear pink.

The other day there had been a funeral march right out front on Louisiana, going up the grassy neutral ground in the middle of the street. The heavy music, the umbrellas, the slow, jerking dance, the people staring ahead beneath their hats. In New Orleans they buried people in chapels aboveground because the earth was so wet all those bodies would slide around. Imagine them swimming in the soft mud, a stiff old foot getting stuck in a gutter.

What did it mean, then, not responding?

Better, anyway, that he didn't know.

Oswaldo said goodbye to Lucinde at Marco Polo and watched as she rolled her bag in through the airport's glass doors, and away. He idled at the dock after she was gone, gazing bleakly about him; he picked up a little pumice stone bobbing on the water and put it in his pocket, for comfort. Then slowly he piloted his boat back over the lagoon. It was a dull, heavy, cold day; he was already exhausted. And now Lucinde was gone. Oswaldo's old British inboard motored slowly over the gray water, past small islands, piles, birds perched on top. Although one might expect him to have a gondola, too, he could not endure them, hadn't for years, hated the sensation of sinking into the rocking black thing as if into a hearse. Long crests of water traveled behind him, breaking gently upon palisades as he passed.

When he got home, he stepped from his boat onto the wet matting of seaweed and looked up at his house. Appalling. It tilted and cracked; salt ate at the foundations; algae slinked up the walls. Inside, it was dim, submarine, and the marble wainscoting, he noticed, had permanently greened. Oswaldo went upstairs to his bedroom, sat on the bed, and kicked off his loafers. Perhaps it was the dripping that made the place seem so *sotto*, he thought, even upstairs on the first floor. All this dripping; it could drive one mad. Like living in a cave. Stalactites. From *sta-lasso*, drip, while *thalassa*, so similar, was the sea; and *thalame* was a place to lurk, while *thalamos* was a bridal chamber, or grave.

He looked at his wrinkled crimson bedcover and thought of how expensive such a thing once was: crimson had been the stuff of kings, the rich pigment itself crushed from murex. How expensive many things once were, how dearly one might pay. He could squint his eyes and still hear the creaking of ships centuries before, sense that quick covetousness as the goods were unloaded. Silver and gold from Bukhara, carpets from Turkey, cotton from Cyprus, lapis lazuli from Sar-i-Sang. So valuable, and having traveled so far! Once cinnamon, cloves, and pepper might even be traded for gold. Yes, how dearly one might pay. He stroked the soft velvet and thought of her who had never lain there, so like his young friend Lucinde, in fact so like his young Lucinde that when he looked at the young woman, he saw that other and allowed himself to imagine Lucinde her daughter, and his. He looked at his hand, at the groomed, ridged nails, at the elegant absence of rings, despite how very rich he was.

Oswaldo sighed, lifting his stiff knees and lying back on the bed, his stockinged feet on the coverlet. He shut his eyes, listening to the sloshing water. He was old, and he ached, and he was tired, yet all the same he felt so restless. Dissatisfied! He stared up at the moldering ceiling, drumming his fingers at his sides.

The problem, he thought then, is this house.

How had he never realized this before? Yes: it was a house like a tomb. Oswaldo touched a fingertip to the wall behind his bedstead and felt the moisture seeping through, the promise of disintegration. Extraordinary, never to have thought this.

For another few moments he lay still, unblinking, his hand limp on the bed at his sides, as the idea slowly kindled. Then he sat up and crossed his arms, wondering. He forgot the pain in his knees and drew them up, staring ahead, his heart beginning to beat rapidly. Well, why not? he thought. Why not?

Oswaldo hopped from bed and hurried in his socks down the hall to the study, his huge desk, the stack of magazines he received courtesy of the Fondazione. What was the name, though? The name she'd said, out there that evening on the boat? He could almost but not quite hear it; yet when she'd said it, he knew he had seen it printed somewhere, that he'd even noted it with a little interest.

It took hours to find the journal with the right article, then to read the article carefully twice and study the renderings and diagrams. He sat still at times, lost in the imaginings that suddenly were so fast and intoxicating that his breath became short. He spent the entire day thinking about it. By night he had decided, had made one or two telephone calls. Then he drew out his gold check-writing pen and one of the Fondazione's official Christmas cards (he always received a few boxes). He thought for a time, then worded his note carefully, and folded it neatly in half. With faint pleasure he omitted the address on the envelope, printing only the name in water-blue ink.

Late that night Oswaldo's motorboat flew over the lagoon, a cold breeze waving through his gray hair. He rubbed the pumice stone in his pocket. So pleasing that such a stone could float, full of tiny tunnels, made of silicate and oxygen, of glass and air. Briefly shutting his eyes, he saw the stone's birth: the explosion underwater, the fantastically slow roiling of water and innards of earth, the tiny pebble making its way over the centuries to find itself bobbing in the lagoon. Pumice from lava, petrified froth. Could one actually build upon it? He rubbed it with the pad of a finger, buffing away a little old skin. He was warming to his idea every minute—more than warming—he was not sure now he could live without it, and he gazed over his shoulder toward the most likely spot as the engine tore up the water.

The boat moved swiftly around the dark fairy city, unclean Veneto vapors hovering beyond it. When he had rounded the Collegio Navale, he cut the engine, and the boat nosed slowly forward like a manatee. He went up the slippery steps and hurried through the park with its spreading pines, the envelope in his hand. The building was one of the newer ones, like a ship, its prow pointed toward the Lido: fitting! Oswaldo slipped through the gate and into the courtyard, opened the door, found the box, and tapped the envelope in.

Anton was sitting in his robe at the desk, marking his students' papers. He'd been up with these the night before until he did not know how late, had finally gone out sometime for air, and had resumed again at six. His coffee was bitter. He was bitter. Bitter and ever more anxious. From his desk he looked out through the pines to the lagoon, the mist, the islands floating on the edge of the sea. Only two more weeks and it would be over, all this time in Venice left behind like a dream. He turned back to the pile of papers; to his futile drawings of corbels, flutings, cantilevers, plinths; to a neat stack of rejections from universities in seven states and three different countries.

Too much coffee; his chest was pounding.

And what about Josephine?

She hadn't answered the last few days. The anniversary had come and gone, and he didn't even know if she'd gotten the flowers.

It was seven o'clock, midnight for her. It was always the middle of her night.

Anton got up from his desk and showered, then stood wet and cold before the mirror in the narrow, long bathroom. He wanted to talk to her! He was sick of this, sick; he wanted to go home. But then what? When the spring semester began, he was finished. What had he been thinking, that something would simply happen in Venice? How could he be nearly forty years old and imagine such a thing? Like a boy going to the beach hoping that the sea would cast up a magic lantern.

He would wake her up, right now; he didn't care. As the phone rang, Anton fixed his eyes upon all the distance the line must travel, down into the stones, through layers of clay and mud, out into the lagoon and then beneath the huge ocean, emerging at last in the bayous.

The phone rang five times, six times, seven. At eight a hot wave rushed through him.

Turning his head, he caught himself in the mirror, there in the dim room, one hand holding the receiver, his face the color of stone, his mouth stricken. A sheet of paper fell silently upon the dusty tile. And as it settled, a little dust shifting, he saw again the surface of the pool, the rings of ripples nudging at his father's wet white shirt and floating tie, the coins on the pool's bottom wavering.

Anton looked up. He still had the receiver in his hand. He put it down calmly and got dressed. Then he neatened the papers, washed the coffeepot and cup, gathered his jacket and black bag, and went out.

One of his neighbors was standing in the courtyard, a newspaper opened between his short arms. He looked at Anton, pursed his mouth as if not to say something, shook his paper, and resumed reading. Anton noticed then a corner of an envelope poking from his mailbox.

Signore Anton Stiers, it said. It didn't have an address.

He looked at the neighbor, who dropped his eyes again.

Something from the owner? Bad news.

But inside was a card with an image: in a deep blue jungle, very lush, was a female form with a pale pink arm bent over her face, a slender, possibly bruised pink arm, fending something off. The sky was dark and complicated. He wondered if it should be familiar, some artist he ought to know. But oh, it looked more like Josephine, in that dark room that day with that tiny glowing maze inside her appearing on the screen. He opened the card.

My dear Signore Stiers, he read. It was written in uneven, watery ink.

Nearly a month since Vera had arrived, Lach still hadn't seen her, and he had to admit he was impressed by her reserve. But she'd forwarded his mail, and the sight of her writing on the envelopes startled him; it seemed to have changed, become slightly slanted. He wondered what that meant, if it meant anything at all. Was she holding her hand differently above the paper, trying to create a different image? Well, why not? He shrugged. He looked at his own writing, wild and hairy along the edge of a sketch, then thought about his chalk sums on the pink house's walls, and wondered if Vera ever pondered them. But at once he saw her as she'd stood before that wall in New York, touching the crack she'd made when she threw him, and he shivered and wound his scarf more tightly about his neck. How did these things happen? How did people go from being adorable to bearing a whiff of the dead?

With the day's mail came a few more things she'd forwarded. Lach noted that the pink house address had been blocked out on one envelope just a touch severely. Had she used charcoal? He smudged it to see. Yes, an angry, bold stroke; he could picture her, picture her dark brows vexed, that full mouth bunched up. All right. He got the point. He'd file a change of address. And truly, he realized, it had been thoughtless of him not to have done this before. Lach shook his head at himself, tore open a bill, and tossed it on the table to worry about later. He observed then that Vera did not seem to have forwarded any mail for Francesca. Now *this* was funny, wasn't it? Had she ever forwarded any for Francesca? He rummaged excitedly through the piles on the dining-room table, on the little chest by the door, and on the dresser. It was true! There were at least thirteen pieces of mail for him, and nothing at *all* for Francesca. Funny. When she usually got most of it. He shuddered a little. So what was Vera doing with Francesca's mail? *Her name?* she'd said, that horrible night. Then she'd nearly eaten it, her eyes unfocused as she held the name in that mouth.

Stalking! At once Lach feared for the house; he saw vandalism, flames, wild headlines. Would she really do that sort of thing? But look at the position he'd put her in! At least, anyway, Miss New Orleans was gone. He'd seen her get into a boat with Oswaldo Manin and a suitcase and had felt a weight lifted from the island.

But now Lach noticed, on the sideboard, one of Francesca's magazines, and stuck to it was a forwarding address label. He felt a little silly. Fine. So Francesca had taken care of it herself; Vera hadn't done anything. Yet.

The next envelope was from the foundation, and he slid his blackened fingernail contentedly through the seal. He enjoyed the little attentions that came from his long association with the place, always the announcements of openings, always the official Christmas card. But what was this? He looked at the card; he held it sideways. It looked alarmingly like a painting of Vera's.

Lach studied it more closely. Pale pink arms, a tiny jag of lightning in an overcomplicated sky. Muscular pale arms, possibly bruised? Was it actually a painting by Vera? He flipped it over. Of course.

Well, how nice, he thought, rubbing his chin. Quite an honor. *Quite* an honor! Lucky girl. The card would be sent to, what, three, four thousand people? And wasn't it funny how some work reproduced so well and was even *improved* when reduced. He placed the card on the mantelpiece, folded his arms, and took a step back, regarding it. Really, he thought, it's terrific, it's great. Really, he thought; I *mean* it. And although he didn't quite put it into words, he had an obscure yet generous sense of balance restored, scales being righted, his blow lessened.

Lucinde's plane reached New Orleans in the late afternoon, the light waning and thin in December, though warm. During the flight she'd stared at the scratched oval of glass, stared through it into the air that was so inhumanly cold. She had gazed down through clouds to sea and tried to calculate what time it was at various points, trying to understand the transitions, where exactly one time zone shifted to the next, and how, in the sea, you would know it. Then for a time she'd considered the shell of the plane, seen it moving, sealed, through all that cold space, and she thought of the airline attendant who had been sucked from a jet. A hole had been blown through the fuselage, and she had been pulled out, just like that, into the silence and the freezing dark. Did she die at once? Did she know what happened? Her body drifting then, lifeless, intact.

Lucinde left faint prints in the mossy pollen as she went quietly up her walk and front steps. Mildew had crept up the door and the walls both outside and in; the edges of a drawing curled. She shut the door behind her, took off her shoes, and looked at her feet, swollen from travel. A clutter of envelopes lay on the floor, and she saw Max's extravagant large writing upon one. She eyed it, standing. A new address. A new address, and nearby— just around the corner, on Rue Royale.

The answering machine flashed hopefully, but Lucinde could already hear the voice waiting inside it; she put out a hand to cover its light. He might as well be curled up at her door, stretched out at the foot of her bed. He hadn't actually come to the house, anyway, or if he had, he'd left no prints on the steps.

Wrapping her arms about herself, Lucinde went into the bathroom, white shells all around the old tub. She shivered a little in the warm air, stepped out of her clothes, and turned on steaming water. Lightly she rapped upon a wall, the plaster soft and damp, smudging her knuckles white.

In the tub she gazed up at the light shaft, where once there had been a chimney. Smoke, light. She often thought of light rising from her chimney and drifting over Esplanade, sending a silent message. She looked in the large mirror, at her pale eyes fringed with blond lashes, and wondered how much she might have promised.

Max knew that Lucinde was back because during a casual evening stroll he saw a light on in her window, and the sight fixed him in place. So now it could begin, he thought; the maneuverings could start. He hurried home, straight to the phone, but then decided not to call her; having sent his invitation, he would wait for a response, which seemed to him more like a strategy.

With still a week before the banquet, he already had a dozen acceptances from people he didn't know, and he was just beginning to wonder what he would do if everyone came but she. Carefully he ticked off names as responses arrived, and each morning, before walking across the Quarter to catch the streetcar to the university, he drank his coffee on the balcony, looking out at the corncob fence but waiting for the clank of the mailman at the gate. Someone who actually worked on a typewriter lived in the slaves' quarters at the back of the courtyard, and the boy who had the rooms downstairs blew bubbles, huge, voluptuous things that wobbled slowly by Max's balcony and up into the sky until they could no longer be seen. Max was known to be the one in the ballroom, which gave him a certain prestige.

When he heard the gate clank this morning, he hurried downstairs with his coffee, bathrobe on and shoes untied, down the stairs whose gaps he now jumped over without thinking. And there it was, in his mailbox: an envelope with his name and the word *Ballroom* printed in her hand. He nudged the cup in the crook of his arm and tore the envelope open with his teeth, spilling coffee through his robe to the tender inside of his elbow.

Of course she would come! She had just gotten in.

Max breathed in twice and looked across Royale at the corn-cob fence. Well, there we were, then. He looked back at the note in case he'd missed something, but the words were all the same. Then he realized that it was a card, so he studied the image for clues: some sort of aquatic blue jungle, a female figure, a languorous rosy arm.

Meaning?

At any rate, it would begin.

Just outside the cave Anton was calling, *Josephine, wake up!* but she couldn't, she'd studied maps and charts last night until almost three, and now it was much too early, the tunnel much too long, because there were miles of them, a hundred miles of drainage canals beneath the streets, and the water made it so hard to walk and the pain in her head was so very oppressive that it was much, much better to sleep.

"Josephine, Josephine! Are you there? I never know where you are anymore. Josephine! Are you dead?"

Dead? Oh no. But—

Here we are, that doesn't hurt, does it? Let's see. Can you see? Up here on the screen, come on, Josephine, up on your elbows. There we are. Well. I must say I don't see much of anything yet. No. Let's have a look over on this side, there, that doesn't hurt, just relax. No, I can't see anything there yet, either. Well, perhaps one little one.

"Josephine!"

What? What?

Look at you, you're gold.

By the time her hand finally reached the receiver he was gone, and she let it drop again. It was quiet then, for a long while. Rain poured down, mildew silently crept up the walls, the cat kneaded along her side. Poor little cat she'd discovered on a branch out-side the window, crying. She opened her eyes once and saw the red light blinking against the window of rain and closed them again under the headache. She did not have a meeting until eleven o'clock, and everyone agreed that she should come in late, because yesterday hadn't she soldiered through interviews with half the engineering school, although by the end she was squint-ing with pain, and then hadn't she stayed so late, typing up all her notes, and then come home and kept on working?

Yes, there may be side effects to the treatment, Doctor Gare had conceded, although his lips pursed primly. I thought we'd gone over that. I thought you knew. Here's a list, though, which might be a comfort. Might not, of course, as well. At any rate, it's information. You can expect headaches, vagueness, despair, he'd said with a wave of his hand. You should probably let me know if you reach that particularly unpleasant item down there at the bottom. Then we'd have to stop.

Are you dead?

No aspirin, no coffee, absolutely no drinking, that's what everyone said. You won't have those things when you're preg-nant, will you? So why not just stop now?

All right! All right! I know.

The windows rattled as a truck roared near, and then the truck seemed to stop. Trash? Today? Of course, today was Tues-day, and Tuesday was when she was allowed to sleep in because there was no meeting until eleven. She'd put the trash out last night, hadn't she? Yes, one hand clutching the plastic bag, the other clutching her shattered head, out there in the murky moonlight when she'd finally come home. Now the trash men were shouting something, there was a slow animal groaning, a crunch, and off the bones and old feet went.

Down to the Mississippi? Her sweet love, the poor Mississippi? To join all those silent female eels, which had already swum, tiny glassy things, all the way from the Sargasso Sea, and still had so far to travel?

A little unusual, yes, that's true, to be producing so few follicles. But it's not too late yet. Another might come. We can always hope, now, can't we? One egg is all we need, after all. And when it matures, we go in with a very fine needle—

Drill right through the shell?

Mmm?

Bedbug, I mean. Bedbug.

Wake up! You've got to wake up.

I do not, I do not, I still have ten minutes!

The phone rang again, and Josephine sat up, her neck and back slick with sweat. But after only the second ring, the answering machine came on. A male voice cleared itself, this time not Anton.

"Josephine Slayter?" he said. He cleared his voice again and began, halting and slightly English. "They said you were not in the office, excuse me. But as the date is coming close and given your part, I understand, in raising the funds to establish the chair, I wanted to make sure you were properly invited . . ."

Anton hung up, irked again. Because he hadn't even told her yet, and until he did, this whole thing would remain unreal. A water villa. He could not quite believe it. *I should like to have a water villa designed and am most intrigued by what I know of your work.* Each time he thought the words, first the whole sentence but then narrowing in on just those two delicious words, he felt a quick melting that ran from his disused loins to his wrists, and he had to clench his fists again.

But the idea was surely ridiculous. They'd never allow such a thing to be built, here, in the lagoon. What was the man thinking? Yet there was in his hand a certain *authority*—more than authority: Anton couldn't think just what. And he was part of the Fondazione, after all; the message had come on one of its official cards. Anton cut the card carefully with an X-Acto blade, and with photo mounts he fixed the halves on a page of his black book: one half with that image, Josephine sleeping with her pale pink arm; the other half with the miraculous message.

He was to speak with Signore Manin in the morning, so he woke early and even showered and shaved and dressed himself properly to be ready for the phone call. This is it, he thought.

This is actually it. His fist opened and closed fanatically with the excitement that kept jagging through him like lightning.

Finally the telephone rang, and a voice that seemed rusty said, "Signore Stiers?"

"Hello!" cried Anton, trying not to sound famished.

"Well, well," Oswaldo Manin said, and repeated what he'd written, praising a few details of Anton's work, flooding him with pleasure. "So do you like my idea?"

"Of course, Signore Manin! Of course."

"*Oswaldo*, please, *Oswaldo*. So many intriguing possibilities, no?"

Anton nodded wildly in his room. So he truly meant it, then?

"Although you should know," said Oswaldo, "I'm still looking for the site."

At that Anton froze. The line seemed to go dead.

"Not to worry!" Oswaldo laughed, a laugh full of confidence. He lowered his voice. "I happen to know of a few developments, a *barena* or two—you know, a sand flat—and a few small islands with ruins that are being considered for building. And there are some old favors due. You see. Not to worry! Difficult, but by no means impossible. And of the idea itself, the villa, I am absolutely certain."

"Wonderful, wonderful," said Anton, his crossed leg jogging quickly. "Then perhaps, Signore Manin—"

"*Oswaldo*. Please."

"Perhaps, Oswaldo, you could tell me just what you are considering?"

"The principal thing is: a villa. In view of the city. And directly on the water."

"Yes, yes, yes," said Anton, scribbling.

"*Directly*, I mean. No sign of land beneath it, no mud."

"Of course not," said Anton.

"*Bene!* There are sites that will come open, as I said. We will have a look. I expect you know the requirements about depths and channels and waste and piles, et cetera, et cetera. So. When shall we meet? *Lunedi?*"

"Monday? Next Monday?" Anton's mind went blank, and he hurried through the pages of his book for his calendar. "Oh no, I'm so sorry, I must go home. I nearly forgot." He laughed stupidly. "Christmas."

There was a dull silence. "Already?"

"And my wife," added Anton.

Another silence. "Christmas, wife. Yes. Well." He cleared his throat. "I have so little time, you see."

Anton tried not to panic. "But surely—"

"Yes, yes, yes," said Oswaldo. "Of course. Christmas and wife. I understand. After the New Year, then. *Auguri!*"

After hanging up, Anton remained sitting, his hand damp upon the receiver. He got up, went to the balcony door, came back, sat down, made a note. Christmas, wife. He looked out at the misty lagoon. He wanted to be in a boat this minute. He could already feel villas congesting his blood and did not know how he could possibly wait until after New Year's, how he could possibly leave.

He looked at himself then, aghast, in the mirror. What are you thinking? He glanced at the phone, but again, it was three o'clock in her morning.

He stood still. Then he realized that he had to go out at once and pick up his plane ticket. He would see her in less than a week, and he could hardly wait to clasp her and crush her lissome limbs. Anton skidded down the stairs and out, feeling the coat's weight upon his shoulders and the comfortable sling of the fine trousers upon his hips, and again he saw himself from above, on his map, which would soon have upon it a faint little blue sketch of the water villa that he, Anton Stiers, was to design, and suddenly he was nearly sundered with happiness, with a warm liquid sense of richness, potency, gold.

The streets of the Quarter were wet when Max went out, wet from the morning hosing, empty and almost fresh. He had been investigating stores for the past two weeks and had made numerous phone calls to specialty shops; this morning he had constructed a complex list, with the items grouped inside different shapes symbolizing different points on his route. First he went to the famous old market, after which he was so weighted down he had to return directly home, drink water, study how well that portion of his list had fared, and then reemerge fresh. Next he went to the Italian grocery stores, heady with olives and crushed garlic, and after that to the A&P. Again he came home, bags hanging from his arms and over his back, and climbed the creaking stairs, panting. After eating handfuls of olives and salami for ten minutes almost without blinking, he emerged once more to mount his new secondhand bicycle and head out into the wilds east of the Quarter. At last he was home for good, stunned; Max dropped the fish and lobster on the floor and fell facedown onto the bed for a snoring twenty minutes.

Then he rose and got to work. Almost all the meal would be Subtleties, but a Futurist version of Subtleties. The first one he'd make was called Love on the Nile. He built a pyramid of sticky dates in a pool of wine and placed around it little cubes of mozzarella stuffed with coffee beans and pistachios. They were meant to be dusted with cinnamon, but no, of course he would not use cinnamon. Love on the Nile: he'd use coriander instead, an ancient Egyptian aphrodisiac. Then he began the Tyrrhenian Seaweed Foam, sea lettuce in waves with crests of fresh cream, little coral-like clusters of chiles, the odd floating sea urchin, plus his own addition, anchovies (aphrodisiac!), as well as a sprinkle of pomegranate seeds. If she ate just a seed or two, he'd have her, then, wouldn't he? He scattered several more. As he whipped the cream, the beaters whirring up white clouds, he gazed into it and saw Io clasped in the cool, vaporous arms of Jove, and Venus arisen from sea-foam. She had told him she liked anchovies, told him most particularly, and surely that meant something, no? Now, Fire in the Mouth. Max rolled dozens of lurid little cherries in a plate of (sadly fugitive!) cayenne, dropped each hot cherry in a martini glass and carefully poured layers of whiskey, then honey, then Strega, and rare alkermes. Heat was important; heat was an undisclosed part of the theme. Pepper was once traded for white women slaves; all of Rome was bought with pepper! The Diabolical Roses he would do later, dropping them battered in the sizzling pan.

And what else to drink? Although he'd resisted medieval things otherwise, he could never resist the drinks; he'd thought about hydromel and about metheglin, but decided at last on Hippocras' aphrodisiac. Along with the bourgogne and the cinnamon, ginger, vanilla, and cloves, he'd certainly add nutmeg, lots of nutmeg. Imagine being an aphrodisiac and not having nutmeg! Which was not only an aphrodisiac but further stimulated intoxication. And now he must turn to the most challenging dish of all, the cockatrice.

Part snake, part cock, with fatal Medusa stare, as it had been some centuries ago? Certainly not. And nothing like the monstrous turducken they constructed here, either. His would be modern and aquatic: part lobster, part turtle, part ray. What nymphs eat, what sirens eat, and that was how he'd lure her, how he'd catch her in his nets. Come live with me and be my love! He could see it now, as the lobsters clattered in the pots and he polished the shell of the turtle and cut the membranous wings of the ray: she would just sit here at the very long table he had constructed, and he'd be first at her left, then at her right, dashing and always at hand, so that her head would spin and she'd laugh and weaken and then—out with the nets.

Max stood up and stretched, looking around his dusty ballroom with its litter of crates. Really he ought to unpack some more. He went to the kitchen (counting the steps until he forgot where he was), got a screwdriver, and pried loose the top of a crate. But the moment the top was off the smell seeped out: the air of the London flat. And there was Therese at the door, her stricken eyes as she realized he'd been there all along, that he'd heard. And Max's party was palled, his plans were disconjured, he sat in a disheveled apartment alone.

Fresh from the bath Lucinde stood looking into her closet. She'd spent each day since returning hunting locations for a particularly gruesome film, and she felt infected by it, sickened. They wanted a shotgun over in Algiers, and some sort of nasty corner in a project like the Bricks, as well as the usual romantic raised cottage, just the right place for decapitation. Hush, hush, sweet Charlotte; Charlotte, don't you cry. She'd had to picture blood and body parts all day, just how they'd best be strewn. Standing before the closet, she didn't move, didn't touch any of the dresses and blouses and capes and costumes that hung there, but simply looked at one after the other, imagining, rejecting.

So, Max lived in a ballroom. There were plenty of ballrooms around, and she'd had plenty to do with lots of them, certain ballrooms that were always reliable. Although it had been some time since anyone had wanted to film anything so old-fashioned here; it was always junk voodoo, violence, vampires, and whores. *Pretty Baby*, the young girl carried in on a tray. Was she naked? Or under a veil? Lucinde touched a sleeve in her closet, trying to recall. A very fine veil, at any rate, because surely you saw her thin body, trembling up there on the silver tray.

She thought of the old quadroon balls: all the pretty caramel or coffee or whatever you like girls dressed up in their finest, hoping like their mothers to be not exactly bought, but taken by one of the white gentlemen. Lucinde touched a long blouse she'd always liked but only rarely worn. It was transparent, sheer gray, with a faint silver line running through it. She held it out, slid her hand inside, and watched the light and sheen distance her skin and the veins of her hand, her nails. Possible.

Max was actually here. She still grew vague each time she thought this, vague the way the clear outline of her fingers became pale behind the transparent fabric. The invitations he'd sent were so like him, so bright and cartoonish and hopeful. A fish theme, or something, Futurist. His ringletting hair, his innocent eyes, the strange lines scoring his face; she thought of his teeth and his parrot tongue, how he'd taken her hand so firmly last year, and how at that moment she'd felt—

Lucinde looked again at the transparent blouse, at her hand motionless within it. Up the river not too far was a place with a beautiful allée of trees. Not the *Sweet Charlotte* place, another one, a place that was beautiful, not haunted. When the rich and clever old planter who owned it was preparing his daughter's wedding, he had special spiders shipped from China, had them spin webs up in those trees. Then he had his slaves sprinkle gold dust in the webs. Such a wedding—can you imagine?—the beautiful bride walking through an allée of trees all strung with spun-gold webs.

Of course her own father had not been clever or rich. Money had been the problem. Was she seventeen then? Surely a little bit older than that? Strange that she couldn't recall. She never saw the man himself, that old friend of her father's, whole, even now; just glimpses of his round face, pink, yellowed, blurred. His teeth, for some reason she remembered his teeth, seemed to be darkly outlined. Perhaps they were dentures? No doubt he was old enough to wear dentures. He had smiled so broadly when she was presented, the sweat shining on the smooth folds of his neck, on the pink top of his head. Her father had been so pleased that such a fine solution had been found to their problem.

Lucinde hummed and returned the transparent blouse to the rack among all the collars and lace and folds of sheer plastic. She slid back hangers, one by one, until she reached the costume from last year's parade. It was heavy and stiff, covered with tiny metallic scales. Not really sequins, you couldn't call them that. More like fish scales. Although really, she thought, more armorial than—what was the word? She could be ready to say something like this when she came in: much more armorial than ichthic.

The night of the banquet that she was forcing herself to attend because the alternative was becoming too much, Josephine dressed herself decently and took the streetcar downtown. But she was early, uncomfortably early, given that she did not know the host, so she walked slowly around the Quarter until she was half an hour late. From the street then she could see party activity, people drinking colored drinks and swinging their legs through the balcony railing up on the second floor. She hesitated a moment. There seemed to be a sort of sootiness inside her. She breathed deeply, went through a gate and a narrow passageway, and found her way up creaking stairs. Again she paused in the darkness, wavering, but then a door opened at the end of a hall, and music and voices poured out. She went in.

It took some time to secure the host, who was running back and forth through groups of people; his hair was pale gold, and his shirt was sky-blue, so crisp the collar seemed independent, one of its wings flipping up.

"We haven't met?" she said when she'd finally managed to stop him.

He laughed loudly, said something that seemed like a riddle, and handed her a multicolored drink that she carried directly to the mantelpiece, where she took shelter. People seemed to be in costume or else eccentrically dressed, and she wondered how they had known to do that. There were some from the university she recognized but didn't quite know; others looked like they must be from the Quarter. She nodded as brightly as she could to a woman she'd seen on the greens before, and the woman nodded back politely but without a glimmer, so Josephine turned instead to her drink. She had not held anything of its kind for some time. It had layers of lime, ruby, and transparent liquid and looked more like candy than liquor. When she took a hotly alcoholic sip, the colors seemed to flare all through her, burning in her cheeks. For an instant she felt something was missing and looked around for Anton. The host kept hurrying from the kitchen at one end to the balcony at the other, his eyes flying at each passage toward the door.

Josephine decided she had to move away from the mantelpiece, so she made an engrossed perambulation of the table, which was extremely long. It ran from one end of the room to the other, a mad hatter table, and had been (she found when she crouched down to look) made of seven doors laid end to end upon a sequence of crates. The top was a fantasy landscape: a crest of stiff cream formed a glacier down the center, with more of those drinks lined up alongside and a pyramid of dates at each end. Costumed students were serving little white squares of mozzarella, one of which Josephine took, surprised to find a coffee bean and pistachio poked inside. Just then a woman came in like Venus, but armored, and when she appeared, Max checked himself fast in a mirrored column and advanced upon her diagonally. Josephine took a few more sips of her drink and watched until she found a fragment of her own face in a column.

"Please, please!" cried Max. "Everyone please take a seat."

The chairs were all different, and many had a circle of plywood and a cushion balanced over the frame instead of a true bottom. Josephine sat uncertainly, keeping her footing. Near her a pair of women faced each other, one young, the other not; you could slip a glass between them and have a mirror: mother, daughter. They turned to her, and she smiled hopefully; they smiled more decisively back; music filled the space between, that and the glasses moving up and down the long table, as unmatched and unsteady as the chairs. Bottoms up! Sweet alcohol gas hovered over the glasses, and Josephine found herself licking her lips. She fingered the tablecloth, which was in fact not cloth but paper, the same sort found on the padded table, which the nurse always rolled down after each woman, tearing away the sheets splotched with jelly and stuffing them in a canister.

No, it is not ideal, Doctor Gare had admitted today.

Venus sat beside her and turned to her with eyes and lashes that were almost translucent, a candle glowing by her elbow. "Lucinde," she said, offering her hand.

"Josephine," she answered.

"Yes," said Lucinde. "I thought so."

"What was the top layer of that drink?" asked the daughter.

"Alkermes," said someone. "Hard to find."

"Alchemy?"

"Al*ker*mes."

"Doesn't that have to do with insects?"

"Berries, I thought."

"Insects," murmured Josephine. "Kermes."

"From which," said Lucinde, "we get crimson."

"The word?" said the daughter. "Or the color?"

"Both."

Lucinde and Josephine looked at each other.

"I was just in Venice," said Lucinde. "I think I saw your husband. What a shame. Here, try this."

"What?"

"No idea."

"No, what a shame what?"

"You aren't there, too."

Josephine shrugged, looked at the glinting surface of the new glassful, then sipped whatever it was, as Lucinde's clear eyes slipped over her.

"Now I hear there's a water villa," she said.

"Mm?" said Josephine, swallowing heat.

"A water villa in Venice! Imagine. Not at all easy. So many complications, Venetians, you know. But when they want something." Lucinde leaned over and lifted the carafe again, began to top up Josephine's glass. A cherry arced over the table and slipped down the mother's shirt. She looked at her daughter, a brow raised, the lipstick crimson on her mouth. Crimson, kermes, they lived in certain oaks; Spanish moss, Spanish fly, the green blister beetle's crushed wings.

"I shouldn't," murmured Josephine, more heat rising up her ears.

"Oh, just a little one," said Lucinde, pouring.

Just that little one?

But why not more?

He'd shrugged. Who knows? Many things we really don't know. Unwilling, I suppose.

Poisoned?

Pardon?

"Nutmeg?" said Lucinde. She grated dreamily. "Imagine not going to Venice. Here. I suppose you had no choice?"

"Oh, work."

The pale eyes pondered her as she grated. "Money, isn't it? You raise money?"

"But not for me." Josephine lifted a hand, surprised a little at its size, and moved her fingers slowly. "No, it just goes right through my hands. The money."

"Money does," said Lucinde. "Doesn't it?"

"Everything does, though, doesn't it?"

"More?"

Josephine shook her head, beginning to marvel at the aquatic room, as Lucinde poured.

"Whatever it is. I have no idea. Now, what a wonderful ring."

Josephine's mouth was pleasantly numb, and she licked her lips. Lucinde smiled.

"Yes?" said Lucinde with the carafe.

Josephine looked at the shapely carafe. "Oh, why not."

"Why not!"

The liquid slid down Josephine's throat as down a shaft into ashes.

"Here it is," said Max when students appeared from the kitchen bearing something upon a bier.

"What is it?" said everyone.

"Pretty Baby," said the daughter, and giggled.

"No," said Max, standing up. "A cockatrice."

"Cockatoo?"

"What, Cocteau?"

"Do you know," said Lucinde, "in Cocteau, in *Orphée*, it's the mirrors that let you into the underworld."

"Underwater?" said the daughter.

"Not Cousteau, *Cocteau*."

"That's how you go in," she said. "You slip through the mirror."

"They're not really mirrors," said the mother. "I read that somewhere. Really, they're pools of mercury."

"Mercury!"

"But weren't mirrors actually made of that once? In Venice?"

"They're very clever in Venice," murmured Lucinde.

"Who is?" said Josephine.

"—glass backed with mercury."

"That's who conducts you to the underworld, anyway, isn't it?"

"Who?"

"Mercury."

"So clever."

"What? You dive?"

"Not Cousteau—*Cocteau*!"

"I meant into the mercury! I *meant* Cocteau."

"I know a man who has a cockatoo. He walks it on a leash."

"Doesn't fly it?"

"Like a kite!"

"Which brings us back," said Max, "to the cockatrice."

It was a large thing with broad, flat wings, tentacles, red claws, and eyes waving on stalks. Josephine pushed back her chair, the bottom falling out, and moved carefully between the backs of guests and the mantelpiece. Three doors wobbled before her. One went to the kitchen, it seemed, and one went out. So surely that left just one? Here was the bathroom. She found the doorknob, got in, and pulled it behind her, alone, in the dark. She patted at walls and damp surfaces until she found a switch. Bright green, crooked walls, cracked sink. Her dress came hoisting up, beneath it were her legs, and one pale stocking was run, a wide lattice running up the inside of her thigh. But is it enough? A little one like that? As I said, it's not ideal. And odd. She wavered. She shut her eyes, floated a little, seemed to be on her back on the white-papered table, legs in the air, the lattice leading down toward that vacancy like Iago's shaft of hell—and the handkerchief, the handkerchief!—and what did she mean that they are very clever in Venice? Who is clever? At what? Venetian blind. Jalousie, jealousy. She looked at her wandering face in the mirror. And what did that mean about mirrors? Sitting, then, not quite on the toilet, Josephine turned her ring around and around, wondering if it might unscrew. . . .

Then she was out of the bathroom again, near the table, fingers clinging to the marble edge of the mantel, brushing mistakenly the shoulders of guests. The table paper had shifted, fallen askew, was covered with splotches of jelly.

"Hello," said Lucinde.

She sat on the frame of her bottomless chair. "Aren't they going to put out new paper?"

Lucinde smiled, slowly. "If they need to, I'm certain they will."

"It is usual, you know. Between patients. Guests. *Hospes.*" She giggled.

"Yes," said Lucinde. "I know what you mean."

Josephine twisted and twisted the ring on her finger, feeling herself suddenly full of salt sea. She looked down at her hand. "You'd think it would just twist off," she said.

"Oh?"

"But maybe it's not a twist-off. Maybe we need a corkscrew instead. Is there a corkscrew?" she cried, and she stood up, surveyed the bobbing table, the remaining wings and claws and dates.

The head of Max wobbled forward, little blond wavelets over his eyes, and hovered near the head of Lucinde. Four eyes like lights peered in.

"What can I get you?"

"A corkscrew." She held up her hand to display. "Then I can open it and everything will come bubbling out."

"Will it?" he asked with his smiling white teeth as again she unscrewed and unscrewed.

"Look!" she cried. "We don't need it!" The ring glanced upon her plate.

"How beautiful," said Lucinde. "May I?"

"Oh, yes."

Max's face seemed to come closer. "Perfectly all right?" he said.

"Why, yes," she replied. "Why do you ask?"

"Indeed," said Lucinde, holding the ring up to the candle flame.

"Maybe," said Josephine, "I should lie down on the table?"

"Or maybe," said Max, "you're not feeling quite right? Maybe you'd rather we took you home?"

Then the walls lurched about her as she sank with Max down the stairs, Max, who apologized, something about hydromel, hydroplane, and when she emerged into the air again, voices called and laughed from the balcony, and the yellow lights of a cab appeared, and suddenly there was a high cry—Josephine! So long!—with a shut hand waving, and a rain of rice falling, and Max carefully placed Josephine in the cab and spoke to the driver. Then she was flying forward, rocking on the vinyl. They stopped at last, her head tumbling. She rapped on the plastic window. Money? No, baby, thanks anyway, the gentleman already paid. So long! She waved. Sleep tight!

Sidewalk, steps, door, keys. Keys? Her hands clung to the walls as the stairs rose before her, and at last she reached the top, where it was quiet.

She moved cautiously down the dark hall, swung for the light switch, failed, but patted until she found it. Rice flew from her hair as she turned her head, a brittle shower that rained upon the tiles when she found her face in the mirror. Green shadows under her eyes and cheeks, her tongue sour and black. Red, crimson, the poor little kermes, tiny berrylike things, crushed to leaking blood. But what do you mean, unwilling? Then everything seemed to well up, she began to laugh and cry, her nose and eyes both running, and she heard somewhere in the dark the telephone ringing.

Anton replaced the receiver quietly. It was just past eight in the morning in Venice, and he'd been sitting at his desk since six, having gotten up that early to catch her before she went to bed and to tell her about Signore Manin. But though he had dialed every twenty minutes, she had never been there until now.

He looked out the window, at the first children playing in the park, at their mothers, at the boats passing by, at the cold pale-blue sky. Blood seemed to move sluggishly through his arms. He looked down at his hand and saw he was trembling more than usual, trembling with the cold that had seeped in as he sat. It was not just in his hands but in his jaw and all down his long legs, rattling at his knees. He looked at the colorless Italian phone sitting on the windowsill. Her voice had come from the darkness of the other hemisphere, the darkness somewhere in her body, her head.

He stood up abruptly, pulled a robe over his clothes, and went to the window and stood there. It had been foolish to begin this when he was away.

I'm just *fine*, she'd said on the phone now, her voice off enough to run up his spine.

Fine?

Of *course*, she said, and this time he could hear her weaving, and he felt slightly sick.

Then what are you doing? he said.

What? She sounded about to laugh.

Josephine, he said, go to bed.

A vaporetto plowed toward the Lido, appearing in pieces through the trees. Then a boat skimmed near the embankment, with a woman in a hat standing poised as a bowsprit. The driver stood with one hand on the wheel, his moustache and gray hair flitting.

He knew she wouldn't remember.

Anton had a little cabinet inside him where he carefully put the things like this that Josephine wouldn't remember. It had been some time since he'd had to add anything. And he didn't even quite know that this was what he did; it was just that he did not want to look at the things themselves but did not know how to be rid of them, either. The first one he had told her: her bare feet on the ice. He hadn't known what else to do but tell her, he hadn't known her yet, and besides, she would have known anyway, what with the cuts and the blood. But what she'd said about it in much the same state only a few months later? It could have been anyone, couldn't it? she'd said. It could have been anyone under that streetlamp; it really didn't make any difference. Her tongue had been black, as on that first night, her eyes laughing and dark.

Anton opened the door and went out to the terrace. Fresh salt air! He opened his mouth and let it scour through him. A Greek ocean liner was being piloted in, white and bright blue, with tiny people waving from the tiers of decks as it moved slowly forward, eclipsing the Lido. He imagined the staterooms and halls, then remembered Minoletti's interiors for the *Andrea Doria* and hurried back in to make a note.

Well, what could he do now, anyway? Nothing.

And now the villa. He would again be away.

He shook his head. Just get through Christmas, worry about what comes next later.

Should he take the boat to the airport or the Mestre bus? The bus was much cheaper. He breathed on his chilled hands. Each round of treatments cost several thousand dollars; he wondered if she'd paid the insurance.

After New Year's, then. And that was only two weeks away. He looked out at the water, but in a new way now, scanning for shallows. No, it made more sense to take the boat.

Up the embankment a mile or so, Lach was maneuvering two suitcases and a heavy bag of groceries to the San Zaccaria boat stop. Christmas! It was one of his favorite times; it always had been; he could never understand that holiday gloom. He and Francesca were on their way to her aunt's place in Toscana, and he was humming with cozy thoughts of the little stone farmhouse, the crackling fireplace, the grunting and shuffling of boars in the woods, the smell of grilled polenta. But first they had to take the boat to the *tronchetto* parking lot and pick up her car. The plastic bag of groceries had slid down his arm and was slicing into his bent elbow, so he paused to readjust as Francesca, behind him, talked to a friend, gesturing with a cigarette and her long hair. Lach dragged the things out to the floating platform and checked the boat schedule. It was a cool, misty day, the water calm; the Lido, far across the lagoon, seemed to float on a pale white pillow.

Fata morgana, he thought, squinting, and imagined the Lido turned upside down. What did that phenomenon have to do with, something about refraction, about light? Light bouncing between different air pressures, he couldn't remember exactly, but something like that, so that the image you saw was reversed.

Fata Morgana, Morgana le Fay; she herself, the nasty fairy, was suppose to live in the water, wasn't she? Somewhere in Italy, somewhere south, in a palace at the bottom of the sea. He'd read this somewhere, no idea where. Most likely she pulled men in, all those waterwomen did. Lach went to the edge of the platform and peered down, imagined long greenish arms suddenly darting out and seizing him by the neck, and he giggled a little at the thought of the splash and his shocked feet disappearing, the cold pheasant left bobbing on the surface like a gull. How did he know these things, anyway? Fata morgana, pavonazzo. It sure wasn't as if he tried. So random, ideas and thoughts and encounters! They floated around, and when he chanced upon them, they stuck.

He squatted to look deeper into the water, at the wooden piles wavering a foot or two under, covered with barnacles, algae, tangled trash. God only knew what was down there. What was it that made things cling? Just then he discovered Francesca's stockinged calf only a few inches from his head, and he wrapped a hand slowly around her ankle. But when his hand began to creep toward her knee, she tugged his hair sharply. She was staring out over the water.

"Look," she said. "Is it?"

When he looked up he saw a handsome motorboat, a 1930s inboard, in fact, old Manin's. And who was in it but Vera, Vera with her bitter timing? How much more obscene could it possibly be than that all three of them should be here together? But thank god, she wasn't looking their way. She was gliding by, oblivious, her hand resting on a suitcase.

Well well, Lach thought, crossing his arms and rocking back and forth from his heels to his toes upon the floating platform. Well, my *goodness*, Vera, very well done. Christmas with Oswaldo

Manin? Or at any rate on your way for Christmas somewhere, by way of Manin? Your sad dark eyes and swollen lips—what else could he possibly do!

Well, thank god, at least she wouldn't spend Christmas alone. Lach realized that without quite knowing it he had been troubled, he had been worried about her. And now it was a load off his mind! Now he and Francesca were free to go to Toscana and roast their pheasant and stir their special pomegranate sauce and drink their drinks by the fire. He smiled at her sincerely as she studied him from the corners of her green eyes; swinging the bag with the bird over his shoulder, he stomped heartily in his heavy boots onto the arriving boat.

The morning after the party, rice lay scattered on the floor and a lobster claw sat in a dull white puddle of what once had been Tyrrhenian foam. Max's eyes were pinkish and watery, his hands sticky on the doors that were tables as he pulled himself along the room to the balcony for air, his feet slipping on rice. He wasn't quite sure what had happened; it seemed she should still be there, somewhere. Dates had been rearranged into lines of ants on the table, and bits of urchin squished underfoot. Ultimately there had been dancing, long, slow tangos from one end of the table to the other; there'd been a heavy beating of heels on the doors and a version of something else Latin.

How could it be that she wasn't still there? That he hadn't noticed her leaving? He stumbled over the divider onto the porch, caught himself on the iron railing, and stared, swaying, down at the bright street. How had he gotten here? When did she leave?

Oh, but now Max did remember something: she hadn't eaten, she hadn't eaten a thing. No lobster, no urchin, no seaweed or date, not a single pomegranate seed. She had especially avoided them. Even though he seemed to remember laughing and offering her some, glistening rubies lying on his lined palm.

All she had done was— He worried for a moment and had to hunt for the thing. But then he found it in a glass atop another glass atop a third one on the mantel. All she had done was to take his palm with those beautiful glassy seeds and place upon it that woman's ring.

Up on the edge of the Garden District, Josephine crouched in the bathroom, knocking grains of rice from her shoes into the trash. Still more fell from her hair to the floor, and when she saw this, she saw again the yellow lights of the cab and that hand waving like a pendulum. She put her own hand to her stomach and shut her eyes. Handfuls of rice, the kermes, the sprinkled spice, everything she drank. It stirred in her slowly, vile, and she made it to the toilet just in time, grains of rice pressing into her knees.

And Anton. Somewhere in all of it was his voice. Wasn't it? She seemed to remember the receiver in her hand, her voice saying something as if from deep in a cave, some dark, echoing place that wasn't where she was but *what* she was, falling away inside her. What had she said? She had no idea. What had he said? Did she laugh? She might have laughed. But maybe he hadn't noticed anything? Had she just said he'd woken her up? Maybe she sounded fine. I'm asleep, yes, sorry, fine. Really, I'm just *fine*.

She washed her face and brushed her teeth. Had she laughed? Hadn't she been crying? Was that before? Or after? And he would be home in a few days. When? Had he told her? She went back to the bedroom and looked around to see if by some luck she'd written it down, perspiration prickling the back of her neck, runny yolk and sickness moving through her again, because he'd probably told her, and if he'd told her, she ought to know and not need to ask.

She made herself do things, queasy. Make the bed. Put dirty clothes in a pile.

But was something lost? It always was, before Anton, when she used to do this: her wallet, her keys, her shoes, something. Where was her wallet? She panicked and clutched at bottles and wrappers on the dresser, crumpled papers on the night table, stockings hanging over the chair, but there it was, what a relief. But something was definitely missing; she felt it, something even more wrong. She found her shoes, she found her purse, clearly she had her keys. Then she realized: her ring. Her hand looked just as it had before Anton, bare and unowned, not even a ghost of that ring on her finger.

That day on the beach she had only looked up at him, her eyes stinging in the sun. But you don't know about me, you don't know.

She couldn't manage it, couldn't possibly manage it, calling that Max, Christmas, this problem, herself; all of it slid down around her knees.

And something about a water villa? What had that woman meant? Did that mean when he came home, he wouldn't even stay?

Lucinde woke early, clean and dreamy and detached. She'd left Max's in the middle of the dancing, gone home and soaked in a hot bath, and between that and a deep sleep, all those heels pounding down the table had been silenced. Max himself had been flushed, with both his blue collar wings flipped up, although she had smoothed them down with a finger just before she left.

In her white nightgown Lucinde moved about the house, tidying; Vera's flight was due in at one. It was such a good idea, she decided as she neatened the guest room, to have invited her. Because what would Vera have done at Christmas, all alone in Venice? Her hands had been so cold, not just outside that evening on the *passeggiata*, but later, too. Those green veins made her wrists like marble, made her seem valuable. Lucinde told her so, but Vera's dark eyes had seemed to shutter, unable to register light.

She was glad she had reminded Oswaldo of Vera, glad that he was taking an interest—glad that he was taking an interest in anything, given how despondent he had been. Something marvelously grotesque about those saints of hers, he had said on the phone the other day, while Lucinde fingered the Christmas card. He always gave her a box.

And now he was thinking about a villa! Lucinde wondered if she herself had inspired the idea and decided she partly had. Or at any rate given him the name, sheer chance that she'd even remembered it. But what was he thinking? They would never allow it. Although Oswaldo did manage these things; he was such an ancient old merchant, with so many invisible strings in his hands.

Lucinde went to the linen closet and took out a pair of sheets. In the guest room she unfolded one, tossed it open on the bed, and waited for its slow billows to fall, gently pressing the air pockets smooth.

She wondered how long Max was likely to wait.

How long had he waited already? Since they'd met: just over a year. Since he'd come: oh, a month or two. Not long at all, when you considered such things. Ten years, twenty; it had been done. There were trials, travails, even thorns, sometimes, too.

And how long would she wait, weaving, unweaving, before she decided one way or the other?

Lucinde smoothed the sheet with the side of her hand quickly, so that the skin slightly burned. What was it that Max had told her last night about sheets, something, but he'd been embarrassed and laughed suddenly, thinking perhaps that it was not proper to speak to her of bedsheets. Saffron, that was it, so precious, coming from the stamens of crocuses; Max had told her that Phoenicians spent their wedding nights on sheets colored with saffron. And anyone who peddled fake saffron, he said, would be burned to death.

Saffron sheets, sheets dyed with crushed flowers. So after the newlyweds had slept in them, were the sheets unfurled from the window, like a sail or a conqueror's flag, as proof?

So, then, how long would she wait? And just what did waiting mean? Again she felt that dreamy vagueness. She gazed at the white cotton, the blue shadows, the long, soft curves. She shook open the top sheet. What did waiting mean? Just doing things. Doing other things in the meantime.

She thought of that funny Josephine. Wild red hair and her tongue so dark, and what did it remind Lucinde of? A certain animal had a tongue like that. She saw again the architect-husband, his face in the bookshop window. So very serious, envisioning his buildings. But what a beautiful ring! An antique fretted ring, white gold; the bright candle flame had glanced through the tiny openings as she held it up to her eye, and Max's smile had danced through the openings, too, as Lucinde watched him print Josephine's address on the paper tablecloth, then take her gently by the elbow and steer her away. Lucinde hurried out to the balcony with the ring, but somehow . . . anyway, she'd decided Josephine would probably just forget it again in the cab. So she kept it and was still standing with it at the top of the stairs when Max came running back up to the party.

Here, she said. You'll have to call her tomorrow.

He looked, she thought, a little flushed.

You will call her, won't you, Maximilian?

Trials, travails, thorns.

Lucinde laughed now, her voice high, and plumped Vera's pillow. Vera and her sad marble wrists. What an ass Lachlan was, and what a fool Vera was to have imagined otherwise.

A few days before Christmas, Anton's cab barreled over the toxic highway from the airport, as Max's had done two months before. He had forgotten about the New Orleans roads, he had barely even been on hard roads in two months, and he clutched the door handle as the cab bounded over potholes. It was still early when they turned down Louisiana and he saw the yellow house. She wouldn't be up.

He unlocked the door quietly and stood at the bottom of the stairwell. The walls near the floor were sheened with mildew, the same old cobweb swaying at the open door. He shut it behind him, lowered his bag to the floor, and remained a moment with his head hanging, eyes shut. Slowly he straightened and gathered himself and began to climb the stairs. Halfway there he looked up and saw Josephine on the landing. The morning light shone from behind, through her nightshirt and glowing copper hair and the golden down on her legs, and that same light seemed to pass right through him, and he ran the rest of the way.

"It was a mistake," he said later, "to do this now."

"No," she said, "really, it's all fine."

She got up and went to the bathroom, the negative glow of her body in the hallway lingering before his eyes.

"So," he said later, "we'll go ahead?"

"Why not?" She shrugged and smiled.

That night they ate downtown in a restaurant that revolved high above the city. By then Anton had told her all about Signore Manin and the villa, which Josephine heard with a look he couldn't quite describe, almost glassy. He reached around the candle and carnation and took her hand as she put down her glass; the lit city slid slowly out of view, and the dark river appeared again.

"Just another month," he said. "Then, if we build, I'll figure something out. I'll go back and forth. Or you'll come."

She smiled and took a sip of her drink, and her eyes drifted to the window. A ferry was leaving the other bank, its lights spreading over the choppy black water. She'd told him all sorts of things she now knew, how some of the levees were twenty-five feet and there were twenty-two different pumping stations, but still it could rain almost five inches an hour, and how the city was both sinking and being eaten by termites. Anton gripped her hand a little tighter, rubbing her knuckle like a lucky pebble.

"Maybe," he said, "I shouldn't go back?"

She laughed and did not bother to answer.

He rubbed his eyes. "But is it worth it?"

Again she didn't answer. And just the sight of that ferry with its spilling lights brought forth the vaporetti, the light glowing from his villa. No longer seeing her, Anton fumbled at his pocket for a pen and began drawing on the back of the menu, humming, until he noticed her left hand on the table.

"Your ring," he said.

She looked at him, and for a moment her glassiness rippled between them, as the room slowly revolved.

"I took it to be stretched," she said. "I don't know, all these drugs, I seem to be swelling." She smiled and turned away to look out the window as again the lit city appeared, then shut her eyes and took a drink. He watched the fine muscles of her throat as the dark river and ferry again came into view, how private she was behind her eyelids.

"I don't know," he said. "Maybe I shouldn't go back."

She sighed. "Of course you should. You have to."

"Then you should come."

She studied him. "And abandon our project?"

"Put it off for a while."

"And then?"

It was true: and then. Return to nothing, not even insurance, start again, time rolling on.

The day after Christmas they had their appointment with Doctor Gare.

"So," he said, rising from behind his desk. "Today's the day. And you're both certain it's what you want to do?" He glanced at Josephine, who nodded. "Fine. You know I just have to ask." He called to his nurse for the specimen that Anton had handed over, chagrined, an hour or so before.

Josephine put on the green paper robe and slid up onto the table; Anton rolled over on a stool beside her and took her hand. Doctor Gare turned on the lamp and lowered his head between Josephine's legs. Anton looked at her slender arm, at the shadows around the green paper armhole, at the shapeless paper smock, at her two bare legs, calves dangling from the bolsters and childish toes moving a little, as they did when she slept.

"There we are," said Doctor Gare. "Easy as pie this time." He stood up and looked at Josephine. "I don't need to remind you, do I?" he said, smiling a little. "Of course we know the odds aren't good. But all the same, positive thoughts." He touched her on the head, shook Anton's hand, and went with his nurse from the room, turning the light off behind them.

It was peaceful then, just the sounds of traffic, the slow shiftings of light. Anton rubbed Josephine's knuckle until she turned her head and looked at him, dark red hair on the paper, and gently drew her hand away.

The nurse came in and turned on the light. "That's enough. You can go."

When Josephine stood up, Anton couldn't help but notice that nothing ran down her leg, the whole thing invisible.

The day he was to fly back to Venice, after they'd said goodbye and Josephine had gone to work, Anton wandered through the apartment, the first time in months he'd been there alone. His plane didn't leave until two. In the bedroom he gazed at the temperature charts still taped to the walls, at that oblivious red line wavering on, as high as his chest, as her chin. In the study he looked at her papers on the desk, her notes for proposals, with articles, diagrams, sketches of levees and detailed maps of the Quarter. She'd drawn a section of wall precisely, as well as a section of some sort of insect with an enlarged pale head. On other sheets she'd drawn the delta, with blue lines of meandering water and diagrams of gastropods, bivalves, eels. She seemed to use private codes in her notes, pictograms as well as words, and meticulous insects were all over the margins: what looked like an aphid with another aphid inside, what seemed to be a spider in a bubble. He turned a page to a printout. Foundations, alumni; she'd raised nearly a million.

He went back to the bedroom, folded his last clothes, laid them in the bag, and zipped it up; he took the two coffee cups to the kitchen and washed them. He stood still for a moment. The apartment seemed empty. He decided to take a walk.

As Anton reached the bottom of the stairs, he saw an envelope lying on the floor. It had not been delivered by the post but by hand, and for a foolish moment he was confused, felt himself back in Venice. But Josephine's name was printed on it, in a large, looping hand. He looked at it, then picked it up. *Sorry to keep this so long!* it said. *Max.* Through the paper Anton could feel the ring.

It seemed very bright outside, and he squinted and stumbled over the broken sidewalk. He did not know what to do. He walked up to Saint Charles, and when a streetcar stopped, he got on. The breeze in the window smelled of electricity, and live oaks went by, and ruined buildings, and a gliding old black Cadillac. He drew out his book without thinking, for comfort, and stared at the calendar, at the pale pink arm, at the note from Signore Manin. He became aware of the man beside him looking over at his book and hunched a shoulder protectively, but just then the man sneezed explosively, and Anton clapped shut his book and got off.

As the sky began to grow dark with clouds, he walked home, working it through with every step, so that, by the time the first plump drops splashed to the sidewalk, he had convinced himself there was nothing to think, nothing more than just what she'd said, she'd taken it somewhere and now it was back. He hurried inside for shelter.

The streetcar went rattling on, dying at the stops, then wheezing back to life, and Max stared out the window. In the space of one block, the bright day faded and heavy gray clouds appeared from nowhere; by the time they reached Lee Circle, drops had begun to fall fast. All the streetcar windows were slammed shut. Max continued staring, no longer out the window but at it, at his own blurred reflection.

Of course he didn't know the provenance of the thing, he told himself as rain sheeted down the glass. He didn't know the source of the image upon that card Lucinde had sent him; it could have come from anywhere, have any sort of promiscuous past, and therefore it made no difference at all if some tall, arrogant black-haired man owned it, too, valued it, too, valued it in fact so very much that he had carefully taped it in his book. Max had glanced over that busy arm, down at that blue-veined long hand, and been shocked. He nearly thrust out his own jealous hand and snatched out the page, tore off the card, and turned it over to see what was written. But then the world had wobbled before him as his nostrils began to twitch, and the image, the black book, the glaring eyes had exploded in his sneeze, and when he recovered from behind the handkerchief, all of it was gone. He saw only the satchel banging from the graceful broad back, and the swing of the long, costly coat.

Max stared at the passing buildings, tumbled wood and cinder block, and at his forsaken face. His hair had curled even more in the moisture, pale blond quiffs above his lined brow, and he lifted a hand to smooth them. His cuff, he saw then, was frayed. Looking down at his sleeves and shirtfront, all he could see was London's dim age. Mismatched buttons, one of them dull and chipped like an old tooth. Max looked back at his reflection. Cyclops. Shaggy, in his shaggy cave: *Come live with me and be my love.* Who would ever want to?

The streetcar was beyond the warehouses now, entering the business district, where handsome polyurethane men sported crisp new clothes in the shop windows. Max's heart quickened, and he sat up, a hand against the window as if to go right through it, right through those other windows, into the heart of the mannequin there. He would have to go shopping. That's what he'd do. He would have to make himself new.

The first day of the year dawned beautiful and cold, light slanting through the water, clear green. When Oswaldo switched on the boat's engine, he was thrilled as he hadn't been for ages by the purr, and as he headed out to the lagoon, he looked around with that old acquisitiveness. The cool air made his blood quick; he had done without this for much too long.

And that was the principal difference, wasn't it? Wanting, or not wanting. If you want nothing, he thought, you do not want to live.

His boat sped over the lagoon, along the bottom of the island of La Certosa. Beyond the Lido the sea opened out in a haze of white that to him had always meant distance and prospects. He thought about all that had once sailed here from over the waters: vermilion, serpentine, lapis lazuli, and silk that would sometimes be so subtly woven as to have the look of the sea, moiré, or to sparkle like the paths of fireflies. And gray marble from Marmara, black marble from Egypt, *marmo greco fiorito*, marbles that looked like petrified life, like columns of fixed, moving water. And aside from that, terre verte, which was made of olive earth, and bundles of the softest brush hair taken from Siberian minks or red Tatar martens, and indigo all the way from the islands that were almost named after azure itself, islands that lay at the violent rift between his continent and that other one, far to the west . . . Oswaldo looked in that direction now, as if he might see through the Veneto vapors, see through leagues of air. Sometimes he still enjoyed the notion that far to the west it all dropped away, Hercules' bowl falling over a ridge of water. The fact that dusky blue dye had come from those western islands seemed to him so fitting; it was the land of the setting sun. Whereas gold had once streamed like the sun from the east.

Yes, he would do it, he said to himself. He turned again and, feeling substantial with a sense of riches, of purpose, let the warmth of the sun fall upon his old cheeks.

As soon as Anton reached his apartment in Venice, he dropped his things, showered, shaved, and went straight out again. He would meet Oswaldo Manin in just three days, and there were so many things to look into he couldn't possibly rest: he would have to collaborate with someone registered here, someone to sign the drawings and get the approvals—most likely it would be Robert—but he would certainly not say a word about anything until he knew where he himself was. And that meant, right now, looking into sites.

It must be on the water, really on the water, alone, not just along a coast. As if it were floating; Anton had secretly begged for that, but Oswaldo seemed not to have imagined otherwise. So, he must find those small abandoned islands Oswaldo had mentioned and, if not a small island, then a little *barena*.

Anton took a vaporetto to the Giudecca and walked to the far edge of the island, to the naval shop by the boathouses, where he thought he could get a good maritime map. But they had none there, and the salesgirl had no idea where he might get one. It was nearly lunchtime by then, the bookstores shutting, so Anton decided to take the Number 20 out to San Lazzaro. He stood outside the cabin with the pock-faced pilot and studied the water as he had never done before, scanning for small undeveloped islands, the slightest traces of shallows, of land. The pilot took an interest and told him where he might find a map, so as soon as he was back on the *fondamenta*, Anton hurried to the place, by Piazzale Roma, but it was closed for the rest of the day. He stood there, chipping paint from the wall. Then he went into a bar and had a *tramezzino* and coffee and decided to go out to the Lido, although he did not want the site to be on the Lido, but from there at least he could take a boat traveling the length of that island. He would have to come tomorrow for the map, and he felt almost a quiver at the thought of seeing the underview of Venice, its slippery bottom stripped bare.

From the Lido Anton boarded a large boat going north, on whose cold upper deck he sat with his camera and book, documenting, taking notes. The boat passed bright hotels, villas, and private docks, until gradually the shore was nothing like Venice but was ordinary coast, with water grasses, scrubby trees, and mud. They passed between Sabbioni and Erasmo and chugged slowly on, north to Tre Porti. Men and boys seemed to stand on the water, bending and gathering mussels; long-legged waterbirds peered into the shallows; every so often one slowly gathered its wings and flew.

At Burano Anton had to change boats, and when the next one came it started to rain. He took a seat inside the foggy cabin and kept wiping the window to look out. But there were no bare small islands. What had he thought, that one might be somehow undiscovered? Here?

Anton shut his eyes and in the dark watched an image slowly emerge, an image of a baby island. They did exist; he'd read about them. Brand-new things that rise from the sea, all wet and clean and hopeful in the sun.

For a moment Josephine's ring hovered before him. He did

not know what to do with it. He waited until it fell away again, deep inside him, until it nestled in the darkness, waiting.

That night he dreamt of the penguins in the London Zoo, waddling back and forth in their tight black skins upon the ribboning ramps. And he dreamt of Josephine, underwater; he touched her blue hip with his fingers and tried to grasp her, to kiss her, but she only smiled and drifted away, her silver tail hanging curved in the darkness.

The next morning Anton bathed and shaved himself cruelly, then took the boat up to the map shop. By ten-five he had it, a maritime map at 1:10,000, and he hurried into a bar and shoved aside the ashtrays and pots of sugar to unroll it. There were some possibilities; he heard himself breathing as he bent over it, intent. It was all so much clearer now, with this map, the lagoon's topography exposed. The marshes and mudflats were olive green, but land and *barene* were pale yellow; he combed the map for tiny yellow shapes, anything bare of a black-outlined building. It had to be within sight of the city and near one of the deeper canals, not part of a long tongue of mudflat and grass. No, the villa must be right on the water, hovering slightly above its surface or emerging from it, clean. His finger traveled over the map, over all the contours of the lagoon floor, the deeply dredged trenches, the little blue rivers that meandered through grass. Then he saw, in view of the Fondamenta Nuove, between Le Vignole and San Michele, a slim yellow crescent at the curve of a deeper canal.

Anton grabbed a napkin, uncapped his pen with his teeth, and began jotting, sketching, even allowing himself a first little villa, knowing now suddenly which way the place could be oriented, given the sun, the currents, the routes of boats, which way to be turned and opened. Because the shape of the *barena* itself echoed the shape of— He closed the napkin in his black book, paid, and hurried through passageways and over the bridge to the Fondamenta Nuove, where he waited impatiently for a Number 21. Then he took a seat on the left, staring hard as the boat plowed through water, staring through the water now, knowing its slippery bottom, its silty ridges and bumps. Slowly the boat went past San Michele, arched around, and pushed toward Le Vignole. And there, at the bend, he saw it: discrete and clean-edged, a few feet above water, was a slim golden crescent of sand.

The idea had come to him as he peered into the water from the San Zaccaria dock. Only two weeks later, Lach had an impressive collection. One wall of his studio was lined with buckets of shells and barnacles, as well as piles of the more formally interesting types of trash, all the things that washed up onshore, attached themselves to piles, or lined the edges of embankments. He had gone out to the Lido in his boots and been excited to discover that in the winter the shells were not plowed under as they were in the summer (to spare soft Venetian soles). The shore was covered with shells, a generous layer, thick and crunching, heaved up by the waves. There were delicate yellow scallops, mussels, even tiny gastropods. Lach kicked through shells as deep as leaves and gathered a representative bucket.

He rode boats around and around the islands, looking at all the edges. He was especially fond of one stretch of embankment, at the northwestern end of the Fondamenta Nuove. There, in a little forgotten inlet, all the empty plastic bottles of the lagoon had converged, bobbing lazily in the shifting water. They were like a herd of seals, he thought, companionable, rocking and nudging one another, and when breezes passed by their open mouths, they sang. Lach photographed the ensemble of bottles as he took the boat past in one direction. Then he got off at the next stop and boarded a boat going back and photographed the bottles again. He hadn't decided yet if he would reproduce the ensemble or model something upon its pattern, but the pattern, in any case, seemed important, the very fact that there *was* one. That so many bottles should wash up just here! It seemed, somehow, affectionate.

Then all the algae suddenly seemed exciting: their relative silkiness or spikes, the shades of green or purple, the different depths at which they grew, how they moved in the water. Lach photographed embankment stones worn yellow as teeth with mossy kelp swaying from their roots. Near the Collegio Navale he'd found a set of steps leading down to the water. The top one was mostly clean, but the next was faintly veined with green, the one after even more so, the second to last lush and mossy, and spectacularly, the final step, underwater, was flowing with bright red kelp. On the Zattere, Lach had nearly fallen into the lagoon as he leaned out over the embankment to get the light right behind some brilliant, streaming green hair. The hair of Fata Morgana herself, he thought happily, just as sirens were manatees.

Now he was carrying a sack of assorted finds over his shoulder, his camera hanging around his neck, as he walked down the *fondamenta*, wondering how he could get into the area behind the Arsenale, where it seemed so rustic. He stopped and looked out toward San Michele and wondered how deep the water was; you could never tell from the color. He turned slowly, squinting, and looked at the horizon, from the cranes and smokestacks of Mestre all the way to the hazy sea. A fishing boat skimmed by as he stood near the sloshing water, a dog alert in the wind at its prow. Another boat followed with a boy and girl huddled together at the wheel. A third boat slowly circled. It moved around what seemed to be nothing, and then the engine was cut off, and it idled. The men on board stood close together behind an opened map, and when the map was lowered, he saw that one of the men was Manin. The other one, too, looked somehow familiar. Lach wiped his nose with a fishy hand and peered a little closer. He had seen this man: yes, in the shopwindow that nasty evening, standing near Miss New Orleans. In fact, he recalled now with a little pluck, he'd seen all three together: Manin, this dark fellow, and New Orleans. They hadn't even seemed to know one another then. Funny! he thought. Just like his plastic bottles.

He heaved his sack of shells and trash a little higher on his shoulder, looked down at the paving stones, out at the water. Actually, he thought, a map would be useful. Although better would be some aerial shots of the lagoon to see how the canals fingered their way through the grass flats, how the little channels wormed through the mud; he'd seen it each time he'd flown in, amazed. Surely somewhere there was a book. Or maybe he should just rent a plane and a pilot and take the pictures himself? More fun.

So had she introduced them? Useful, Miss New Orleans. A man could arrive in Venice and within a month be in old Manin's boat, in his circle.

Two more days at the little house near Biloxi, then back to New Orleans. Lucinde and Vera had read and gone for walks and worked a little and left each other alone. With the clean sand and clean air and sunshine it felt like another season, and another century as well. Two ladies at a seaside house, away from complications.

Lucinde was placing oystershells in a meandering pattern around the edge of the terrace. Oystershells, mother-of-pearl. This pattern she was making was the kind Max would enjoy, like the cresting wave of cream on his table. She could see him now, his long pale face with its premonitory lines, his hopeful eyes, those hands that seemed always to hover about her but that she had so far managed to evade.

But what do you really know about me? she asked him sometimes on the phone. With the luxury of distance, just his voice with its curious depths and haltings; a voice that, though weightless, she could hold tentatively in her hand; a voice whose very immateriality she invested with secret shape and color as she heard it in her mind in the darkness when she rocked to sleep, she could almost imagine—

But then, but then. She looked at her hands. Sometimes she marveled that they were so closed, that bodies were almost completely sealed. She turned her hands over, and shut her eyes, and took a careful breath.

Lucinde placed the last white shell and stood up. Shielding her eyes, she looked toward the sea, then glanced over at Vera, who had been absorbed in her watercolors at the terrace table but now lay in the lounge chair. She could work for hours, peeling off the sheets of wet, bright paper and dropping them like petals upon the flagstones around her. When she worked, her teeth appeared between her lips, sometimes taking little bites, and her eyes drew an invisible channel between herself and the paper. Finished at last, she would look up, blank, her face avocado-pale beneath her broad hat. Then she'd falter to a lounge chair and sink.

Lucinde sat down with a glass of water and looked at Vera as she slept. In the sun her hair spread out like a dark pool, and her large, soft lips fell slightly open. A thin line of liquid formed in the crease of her stomach, a tiny pool in the hollow of her neck. Lucinde thought of a woman she'd read about who'd died sunning on a foil sheet while she slept. She baked. She was warm when her husband came home and touched her, and so she seemed asleep, until the sun went down and the air grew chill and still she simply lay there. Right in the middle of sleeping, Lucinde thought, one kind of darkness gave way to another. Would she have noticed it at all? Was there any transition, a shifting, a clue? Transitions like that were so hard to fathom, one kind of unconsciousness leading to another. Did she grow extremely hot, but not even know until it was too late? And once she was dead, did her body continue to sweat? Of course even inanimate things sweated, a piece of fruit, a sandwich in a wrapper, tiny beads of moisture rising, the first hints of dissolution.

Dissolute, absolute. A little trickle appeared at the corner of Vera's mouth, and the oil and sweat on her skin glistened, melting. As she must have melted into Lachlan, simply opened up, seamless, mouth liquid, allowing. Like two ripe fruits in a bowl in the sun, skins slowly dissolving between them. And inside Lach, Lucinde thought, if you cut him, if you took a knife and slit him open down the middle, inside that plump pinkness it was all wet black seeds.

She took the glass of ice water and held it in her hand; then without sipping it she pressed the cold glass to her forehead. After the little shock of cold it was pleasingly painful, then numb. She held the glass there until the numbness gave way again to ache, an ache deep inside the bone. Shivering suddenly, she put the glass back upon its wet ring and got up and went inside.

It was dark, her eyes still dazzled by the brightness. For a moment she stood, dizzy, but when her eyes adjusted, she went down the hall into the bedroom and without thinking crossed the soft carpet to the mirror as one might approach a window, or a friend. She felt comforted there, as always. She gazed privately into her eyes, thinking to herself, at length. This wasn't really vanity, though. Or only in the largest sense of the word.

When Max learned that Lucinde would be going to Biloxi, he took the information in calmly and told himself that another little pause would be perfectly fine, that it indicated nothing decisive. To tell the truth, he was relieved; the banquet had blazed like a fire that needed to die gradually away, be forgotten. Too garish, too obvious. Although it did seem to have won him renown on campus. He smiled energetically whenever he was hailed on the greens and crisscross paths, rising a little on his toes and trying to lock those friendly faces in his mind.

A reprieve was just fine; Max had things to do. On the third of January, for instance, he was going to have a haircut. This was something—regular grooming—he had never properly managed in London, looking on with despair as wisps of hair sprouted not just from the sides of his head but from his nostrils and ears as well. It was always a revelation to go to a barber and find that he could be shorn new, that he could actually be made trim and fresh; each time he went, he promised himself that he would make it a habit. It had taken some time for Max to find a barber in New Orleans, a good old-fashioned barber, as stylists with their music and gossip made him nervous. But at last the bib was fastened around his neck, the scissors began their work, and he shut his eyes, soothed, feeling bits of sorry London snipped and falling to the floor.

After the haircut Max went shopping, vicariously at first. Each day, as he walked through the Quarter to the streetcar, he studied shopwindows and the mannequins inside them until he had imaginatively constructed how he should be. Bright; everything bright but not too bright, everything fresh and new. He felt very smart, excited, as he stood before mirrors with the salesladies, who took an interest in him and his venture. He left the shops after hours of exertion, with a mustard-colored shirt, fine flannel trousers, a jacket of periwinkle blue, new half boots with buckles, pink socks.

Then, back in the ballroom, Max put on all his clothes to test them with his new haircut. What a wonderful thing new clothes could be! What a difference they could make! He could see the effect only partially, given the size of the bathroom mirror and the fragmentation of the mosaicked mirror columns, but still he could feel it, the creaky solidity of new shoes, the crispness of the shirt's lines, and inside the trousers his very skin like a baby's, clean and valuable and new.

It began soon after Anton left, the gaudy signs and masks in shopwindows, the magenta and gold streamers flapping from telephone wires, the king cakes with their green and purple icing brought in each day to work. Josephine took her slice on a paper plate and bit gingerly, her tongue searching for, and hoping not to find, the little plastic doll baked inside. Her colleagues' mouths were chewing with care, throats slowly swallowing, the bow tie of the chief of foundation relations bobbing up and down.

"Anyone got it yet?"

"Who got the baby?"

Earrings glinted as heads were shaken, and paper napkins dabbed at the corners of lipsticked mouths and were balled up and thrown away. Then all eyes turned toward Josephine. Her own eyes wandered away, but there was no avoiding it; the click of her teeth against the thing could be heard. She swallowed the cake all around it and sucked it clean before fishing it from her mouth, the plastic baby with its little kicking legs and outstretched, miniature hands.

"Josephine again." They sighed.

"Josephine always gets it!"

In her office she opened a desk drawer and placed the baby be-

side all the others already lying there, as if in an orphanage.
Taped to her desktop was a calendar, and what it said to her as
she stared down at it was, Why not count? Although she'd already done it at home that morning; she already knew exactly
how many days in she was. Twenty-six. And what to make of
twenty-six? Nothing at all. Because it was almost certainly impossible, given the situation. But now it would have to go on
longer than twenty-eight days, since that was the most recent
record to break. And then, even then? She opened the drawer
again, gazed down at the plastic babies, and wondered when they
were dropped in the batter, and why it should be that she had
bitten one almost every day for a week. It means something!
cried all of those women out there, perfectly nice women who did
not know a thing.

Doctor Gare had touched her head gently with his washed
white hand when it was over last month, as if blessing, as if
maybe that would help. Positive thoughts! he said, somewhat
tired.

Twenty-six gave way to twenty-seven, and finally it was day
twenty-nine.

"So how are you," Anton said, the phone meter ticking between them, and what sounded like a pencil tapping on wood.

She had meant to say nothing, not to give false hope, but
somehow the number came out. It took him a moment to hear
her, but when he did, he fell silent, so that she could hear the
hope in his breath.

"But," she said, "I don't think it means anything."

Now he didn't seem to hear her at all, and Josephine could
tell that he had opened his black book and found the page in his
calendar and that his trembling fingers were drawing bouncing
baby circles.

"I really don't think it means anything," she said again, but

the words, as they floated into the air, seemed in their very un-
certainty to belie themselves, to make the whole thing possible.

Just side effects of the shots. She knew. Because the odds of
something actually *working* in there . . . Everything was just al-
tered, her blood all confused.

Although. Josephine looked up from her computer screen,
from the threat of hurricanes and subsidence, from the curious
discovery that some of the levees were actually made of sugarcane, and for a moment she imagined everything different, everything smoothed over, made right. The ring had turned up, after
all. She'd started to cry, crouching there on the floor, when she
came home to no Anton but that envelope at least.

Day thirty, day thirty-one. On day thirty-two Josephine wandered into the K&B on her way home from work. She walked
down the aisle, looking at all the Valentine's Day cards and red
hearts full of chocolates; she went over to the feminine zone, all
the pink boxes and neat little kits, but she just kept walking.

Anton had visited his *barena* three times. He hired a man with a boat and whizzed across the lagoon, splashed into the cold water, sank into the mud, and took pictures before he'd even climbed onto firmer sand. He stood still, shot, shifted his focus a fraction, and shot again, making a panorama. To the east was a narrow stretch of water, piles, and then the trees of Le Vignole; to the north was a seascape with a few islands, the sky; and to the southwest, across the hazy water, lay the city itself, with its famous campaniles and half a dozen cranes. Anton taped the pictures together on sheets of paper, then taped the sheets of paper to the wall. Although he'd been itching to start designing the villa at once—already he saw the light, the glass—he'd held off, wanting to give Signore Manin the sense that he was directing the project. Instead, Anton had been assembling his images of water architecture details, preparing a pastiche of possibilities for their next meeting.

Now he waited for Oswaldo on the bridge to the Collegio Navale. A tall young man with graying hair and a satchel not unlike his own walked by, with a baby girl perched on one shoulder like a little sack of flour. The man held her loosely about the ankle, and her tiny hand steered him by the ear as she gazed down at Anton, passing.

Day thirty-two. Better not to think about it. He shifted his satchel, climbed up the bridge, and looked down at the water. Running a hand through his hair, he let it linger a moment on his ear. It was troubling how little he could see through the water. He looked out toward the Lido, which always seemed to hover on smog or spray.

Signore Manin's boat appeared, and Anton climbed awkwardly down the slippery stone steps. They motored straight out to the *barena*, maneuvered a short distance from the deeper canal, and anchored in the shallows, so that in the cold winter sun, next to the site, Anton could produce his images on cards, one by one. He and Oswaldo stood at either side of a little round table. Neither said a word, Anton laying each card out, Oswaldo considering it and then sliding it to one side of the table or the other with his finger.

When the cards were finished, Oswaldo slid the winning stack before him and fanned it out. *"Bene,"* he said. He squinted out at the water, his long moustache moist at the tips. "Very well. But"—he turned to Anton with a wan smile—"I would so much like a shell."

"A shell?" Shells flew through Anton's mind: an eggshell, a racing shell, a conch.

Oswaldo looked impatient. "A shell, a shell. You know the one. Surely you've seen the pictures, even if they're before your time. The city is often shown on a shell; Venice, Venus, is borne upon a shell."

Good god, thought Anton. A scallop. He reasoned quickly. Maybe a perfectly flat one. A flat concrete shell like one of Nervi's, smooth and white and organic. In fact, he thought next, the whole thing could be a bivalve. Not really a bivalve, of course, just the hint of one; two flat, smooth, modern slabs, their shapes organic and incongruous, and the bottom slab could be cantilevered upon two legs in which all the plumbing et cetera could be hidden, and one wavering wall, following the line of that organic shape, the wall most visible from the city, would somehow be made of or filled with water so that from a distance it was translucent, lagoon green. His palms became wet at once. Yes, the whole thing must be transparent between thin white slabs, water and glass, and there must be a way to project light upon green water in glass to hint at *verde antico* but in fact be nearly its opposite—

He was sick with excitement. He looked up to see Oswaldo regarding him.

"*Stai contento?*" Oswaldo said mildly. "*Va bene.* Then you should proceed. And next time, a few drawings." He switched on the engine, the boat tore up the water, and soon they were bobbing alongside Anton's park. But as Anton clutched his satchel close and lifted a leg out, Oswaldo said, "It could be, you know, that there are others."

Something like a flame went through Anton. Other projects, he thought; my god, it's starting, I might actually do it, arrive! He flushed and looked down at his hands.

Oswaldo was peering at him curiously. He nodded then and drove off.

Only a minute later, as Anton walked under the pines to his apartment, did he think with a shock, Or did he mean other *architects?*

Oswaldo wasn't sure how it happened, but he woke up with a brand-new desire. He stayed in bed an hour or so, trying to fall back asleep, but the desire nudged at him like a cat, and no matter how he twisted or tossed he could not push it away. So he got up and paced awhile in his slippers on the cold, cracked floor, watching the sun emerge through the fog; then he spent the whole morning thinking about it, until finally, after meeting with his Palladio fellow, his architect, he went to the Accademia and the Doge's Palace to acquaint himself with some of the precedents. Then, although really he had made up his mind, he decided to call Lucinde for advice.

As he dialed her number, Oswaldo looked out his window at the sloshing water, at a crooked sign hammered onto a pile. TUBAZIONE SOMMERSA. The sort of thing his Palladio must be sure to know all about. He pictured the numbers he'd dialed traveling across the sea, somehow creating sound. He'd once seen the underwater Atlantic telephone cable where it emerged in Ireland; it looked like a barnacled sea creature, and how extraordinary that it could bear the likes of Lucinde's silky voice.

"I was thinking," he said when she finally answered, "about doing something new."

"You already are," she said.

"Yes, yes, in addition to that." Oswaldo realized he was not quite talking into the receiver and readjusted his hold on the thing. He caught sight of himself in the old tarnished mirror and frowned. "What would you think," he went on, "of a portrait?"

"Of?"

"A *portrait*," he said again, embarrassed.

"I heard a portrait. I meant of whom?"

He flushed a little. "Of me."

"Oswaldo!"

"It's not so vain," he said. "People do this."

"Of course they do. Especially people like you."

"What do you mean?"

She laughed. "People who are rich. And important."

He did not answer; he heard her think.

"Is this to go in the new house?"

"The villa, yes, it's all . . . *tutt'uno*."

"I see."

"I am not," he said, "altering. I am not wearing rouge."

"Of course not."

"Indeed."

"So," she asked then, "have you chosen your artist?"

He was moving his gaze slowly around the room, beyond the old chipped mirror, beyond the green-stained marble walls, to the window, back out to the tossing water. "I am just beginning to consider this."

"But isn't it pretty clear?"

When she said that, of course Oswaldo knew that was what he'd been thinking all along. In fact, he realized happily, it was because of *her* that he'd had the idea to begin with; something had slipped into his head and sunk there, undetected, until now.

He had a brief vision of hemispheres, globes; he saw himself in velvet.

"She'd do something fanciful, wouldn't she?" he said.

"Yes," said Lucinde, "she would. And she just got back to Venice this week."

Lach left his studio and walked to the *fondamenta*, paused when he reached it, and turned left. A drink, he thought; definitely a drink. Because look how hard I worked today! Only one more piece to do before the show. Besides, he thought as he walked past the different-colored shopfronts, much better a drink than go back so soon to that dark apartment when there's all this wonderful light out here. He went to a bar, pushed through the hanging beads, and when he'd ordered, he returned to the doorway, smoke wafting around him, drink in a glue-crusted hand.

He looked down along the embankment toward his poor little house, lit just now by the late wintry sun, the contours of San Giorgio beyond it. Across the water, along the Zattere, the light on the buildings was rose. Lach shut his eyes and deeply breathed the ozone air, the sun cool gold on his left cheek. He imagined the complexities of Venice and its slinking muddy waterways all around him and, toward the sun, the ordinary world with refineries and *autostrade* and trains. He looked up, squinting, the light slanting into the water. A vaporetto was making its slow way toward the dock, and he watched it advance, crests of clear water and froth at its nose. As it drew close, he noticed among the people on deck that hat, that terrible green hat. He pushed away a strand of beads to see better. What, was Miss New Orleans back? No, he saw then, it was Vera. Wearing New Orleans's hat. Well, why not? She wouldn't need it in New Orleans, would she? It hardly ever got too cold there. The boat stopped, and people got off, that hat floating along with some others. Lach leaned against the doorframe and sipped his drink, and he noticed then that Vera, as she came up the plank and over the platform, seemed to have her eyes fixed upon a man a few steps before her, while her hand at her side slowly opened and shut. The man paused before the church, took out a book, and wrote something down; then he disappeared up the steps. But this is too much, thought Lach, stepping forward. First the man appears unknown in a window, then he's riding in Manin's boat, and now, will you look at this?

Before he'd even thought about it, Lach found himself standing clear of the doorframe and waving broadly at Vera. What am I doing? he thought. She peered at him, squinting in the late sun, and didn't move for a moment, during which time he thought of stepping back quickly behind the hanging beads. Then she gathered herself and came toward him like a coot, head down, black wings behind her, with that ridiculous hat. He panicked. By now the man had discovered that the church was *in restauro* and came back down the steps. He looked up the embankment directly at Vera and then through Vera at Lach, who misswallowed his drink and was coughing by the time Vera reached him.

She looked at him, light blanching the side of her face and illuminating the little acrylic hairs of her hat. He smiled in a genuine, friendly way, and she glanced beyond him into the smoky room, then at the blackened nails of his hand on the doorframe. He strummed his fingers, taking a sip.

"So how *are* you?" he said.

"Fine." She did not smile. But he could see something moving around in her eyes.

He gazed at her benignly for a moment, then gestured inside with his chin. "Drink?"

She studied him. "You look like Silenus."

He blinked slowly, looked at her face half lit, half shadowed, and at the green hat.

"Nice hat."

She pursed her lips. "Lucinde's."

"Lucinde's." He took another sip. "I've been trying to remember her name!"

"Lucinde," she said again, as if for protection, and Lach couldn't help but think of Glinda, the good witch, floating by in her bubble. Something spiteful stirred in his mind, caught a little fire from his drink, and, before he'd quite planned it, came out.

"Tall and dark," he said.

"What?"

Lach gestured toward the Redentore boat stop, where that man stood waiting, hands on his hips, staring over the lagoon at the city. "Mister Palladio," Lach said.

She looked at the man and then back at Lach, and without saying a word she nodded and left.

Well sure, he thought later, a hand in his pocket, whistling as he walked home. Well sure, why not? Why shouldn't she look around? She should. Why not? She could. Who could blame her?

Max planned his first excursion to be surreptitious and at dawn, when the streets were wet and hopeful. He hurried along Rue Royale with a Brooks Brothers shopping bag in his hand, and when he turned onto Esplanade he felt a lurch. He did not cross the street as he had that first time but stayed on the proper side, as if by approaching the house this way he might catch it off guard. Tiptoeing up her dusty steps, he held one hand over his mouth, nearly choking with a suppressed giggle and sneeze.

What I think, Lucinde had said on the phone the other day, is that you are indiscriminate.

Indiscriminate! Him! Oh no. He had absolutely selected her.

She sighed. Don't see how, when you know so very little.

I know what I want, he thought, and I know that I am myopic. Myopic, cyclopic, and she is Galatea . . . Whiter than ricotta! Firmer than an unripe grape!

Max tiptoed up the steps, but his feet creaked alarmingly on the wooden porch, its ceiling pale wasp blue. It was critical that she not awaken, that she not catch him when he came, for he was not only the cyclops but the satyr in the woods, stealthily pulling back the sleeping nymph's veil.

Max's gifts were only somewhat subtle. A fine sheet of dried nori seaweed, ordinary enough, but rarely used as paper. This, in-scribed, he slid through her mailbox, watching with satisfaction as the green sheet slipped through.

This earned him an appreciative phone call the following af-ternoon, her voice, as always, like smoke. So, a few days later, he again hurried down Rue Royale, now with a balloon he'd inflated lovingly with his breath and several whispered words and a final spritz of perfume, because he'd read about this and liked it; it was even more subtle than a singing pie. Max tied the balloon's neck with a string, at the other end of which he'd carefully threaded a big needle, and he fixed this to her door handle.

As he hurried away from her house, the back of his neck burned. Had she seen him?

Maybe she had. Maybe she stood up there, by that window, and gazed down as he came and went. Or, given how low that window must be, maybe she lay in some sort of cushioned case-ment, some sort of odalisque chaise longue, idly stroking a tassel or some such as she watched him hurry off. And meanwhile per-haps she herself was idly stroked by some tall dark—

Now not only Max's neck but the tops of his ears grew hot, and he hurried home, determined not to think about, not to imagine, that black-haired fellow with his long legs in his well-made trousers, affixing her card to his private book, pressing it down firmly with a knowing hand.

The air seemed to be changing, Josephine thought as she walked home from work. It was unclean, a little bit restless. Magnolia leaves dropped; banana leaves rustled; everything was dusty and dull. Cars wheeled by, spinning up grit, the trams rattled and smoked when they stopped, and the grass on the neutral ground lay lank. A scruffy little dog stood on the corner and caught her eye, its tail briefly coming to life.

She did not know what to do about these days simply passing. She could not bear to speak to Anton. Days and evenings, anyway, were safe; she stayed at the office until well after dark, even though by five he most likely wouldn't call. But in the morning, when the phone rang, she jumped up, ran to the bathroom, and locked the door. Because what would they do, somehow not mention it, the fact that she'd reached day thirty-two? The center of her body was the center of gravity, and there, in the dark, her heavy brain dwelled, deliberating just when to punish.

Finally, on day thirty-three, she made herself call Doctor Gare. Although she planned to tell him that she knew it was not at all likely.

Come now, Josephine, he would say.

But, Doctor Gare—

Pardon?

I mean, if it's spoiled?

"Thirty-three, you say?" he said when she called, and she imagined him rising up on his toes in his office. "We've never gotten this far, have we? I told you, reason to hope! Hold on." There was a scratching then, a shuffling of paper. "I've got you down now, good. Give it until . . . why don't we say day thirty-five, and then go on over to the K&B and buy yourself a test. And if it's positive, call me at once, and we'll test you ourselves. So that we can start the next step if we need to. Because sometimes, you know, it needs helping along, to make sure there's a friendly setting. They call it nesting, do you know, in German. Nice little term, you can see the thing burrowing. Into the uterus. So there we are. You will remember, won't you? Josephine?"

But it's not true, I'm not, I know it.

Whatever makes you say such a thing?

Why do I have to keep saying it!

Thirty-four. Josephine walked home from work with care. The air still smelled faintly of sweet olives but mixed with something else now, a gassy yellow smell from the refineries. The scruffy little dog appeared not far from the corner, its eyes again hopeful, and followed her partway home.

On day thirty-five, while Josephine was at work, something began to happen. From her internal office she didn't know until the head of alumni relations rapped excitedly on the door. "You've got to come see, come feel this!" The air outside had grown strangely still; the sky seemed to have receded and paled; it was growing very cold. It had not been so unusual at first, fifty degrees or so, but by the time Josephine came out the temperature had sheared away to forty. Yet still it kept falling, the cold dropping over the city, falling and falling, hitting thirty, dropping below, dropping down to ten, to seven. Someone turned on a radio: *Pipes, pets, plants, hurry home!* The office was shut down;

everything was shut down. As Josephine hurried out, the cold struck her in the face with a shock. Ice air, Providence; her throat went dry.

The streets filled with people rushing in cars that seemed harder, more brittle, or hurrying along the frigid sidewalks, or riding with arms wrapped around themselves in the chilly street-cars. The surfaces of everything seemed paler, more northern. Sounds were different, tires spinning dryly over the road, doors slamming shut with a sterile bang, voices thinning in the air.

The cat, the plants! With numb fingers she unhooked chenilles on the porch; she dragged in philodendra and Norfolk Island pines. There was no proper heating in the house, just small gas heaters planted here and there in the floor. She lit them, and soon the place smelled of burning, of gas, faint blooms of warmth hovering around the heaters themselves but not venturing any farther. The glass of the windows seemed to tighten and shrink so that the frigid air crept in, the walls stiff and thin, no insulation at all. *Turn on the taps!* clamored the radio. *Turn them on before it's too late!* So she did, the bathroom sink, the tub, the kitchen, and she kept running from one to the other trying to turn them on harder as the streams of expensive, undrinkable water began to grow thin. But at last they shrank like the windows; they sputtered and ran dry. The pipes could almost be heard cracking, while the palm trees invisibly died.

That evening she sat under five blankets with the cat. It was silent outside, the world foreign and far.

At about ten she suddenly remembered and hurried out and after a while found the little dog shivering in the bushes. She brought him in and put him in the bathroom with a blanket and bowl of water, while the cat stood glaring outside the door.

In the morning the office was closed; schools were closed; almost everything was closed. The coffee steamed Josephine's cold nose but steamed away all its heat at once; she warmed the cat food in the oven. Then she made both the cat and the dog baskets, lined them with old sweaters, put them as near gas heaters in different rooms as seemed safe, and went out to see what had happened.

Everything was pale and stricken, the broken sidewalks now frozen as well, creaking beneath her feet. Frozen ruin was everywhere; shocked greenery had become heaps of gray ice; palm trees stood withered. Only two cars came down Saint Charles as she walked along, her breath puffing into the cold dry air; the faces of the drivers were bitter and pinched. No one else was on the sidewalk; overhead, purple and gold streamers made a tinselly sound in the breeze. As she'd suspected, the K&B was shut, an opened can of frozen cherry soda left on a bench at the bus shop.

Things seemed to have stopped, quiet and dreamlike. Everything seemed suspended, not real. She went down Foucher to Prytania, but on Doctor Gare's door was only a note: *Office shut due to broken pipes—please call this number in case of emergency.*

Oswaldo had given Vera the purest pigments, a slab of marble on which to grind them, and the finest brushes. Several mornings a week he would sit before her in an old velvet chair in his dripping hall while she studied him, although he had assured her at once that soon he would live somewhere else, new and altogether different. She took only a polite interest in this and continued studying him, seeming to see more than enough as it was. Her eyes were dark but almost milky, absorbed, looking at him in a way he found soothing. She dabbed her brush in azurite, the greenish blue of northern skies, and Oswaldo breathed in the smell of rich oil and listened to the sound of wet strokes like tiny oars in water.

Before she came, he'd looked at himself in the tarnished mirror, wondering what she'd make of him. His drooping moustache, salty brows, the fine wrinkles around his eyes. The moustache trailed away to nothing, bluish gray like Tiepolo storm clouds; the folds of skin about his neck were delicate as silk. He studied his eyes. He liked to think there was something of the mariner in them, something that had seen far, squinted off into the promising distance. In one of the portraits he admired, a man's profiled eyes stared off, while beyond him, through the parted gold-edged curtains, the lagoon lay bright, laden with boats, the sea paling away.

"You don't mind," Vera said, her voice a little hoarse in the cavernous room, "you don't mind sitting still?"

"Certainly not." It was like being stroked. More than stroked: made more significant, transformed into something better.

Smalt blue lay in a snaky coil on her palette. She shook her shoulders, shook out her inky, ropy hair, and gazed at the splotches of beautiful pigments spread out like a fan.

Yes, thought Oswaldo. This is what I want. My villa and my portrait. Monuments, *mementi*. He glanced defiantly out the window at the sea sloshing against old foundations. Here, inside, with her thoughtful eyes and enduring pigments, and that soothing warm smell of linseed oil, he felt safe and peaceful, contented.

"I'm having a new place made, you know," he told her once more.

"Yes," she replied, and continued working.

"I have a very good fellow. My own Palladio."

"Yes," she said again.

Then again the quiet, the smell of oil, the dabbings and wet little strokes. Thin light fell through a high window, and where it fell upon the damp floor grew a fragile carpet of green. Oswaldo began to feel sleepy. But just as his head nodded to his chest, he was startled by the ringing of bells.

"Four o'clock!" he cried, fumbling awake. "I'm sorry, it's time for Palladio."

Anton had spent the past week and a half struggling with the Soprintendenza, the Salvaguardia, the Edilizia Privata. Sewage; at least six meters of piling, although probably, given his site, still more; an enclosed septic system; the worries of salt and metal; the threat of electrical storms in June and the attractions of objects on water. He was exhausted from wandering the labyrinths of documents in the Archivio, and his dreams seemed to weight his damp pillow.

When he woke, the thought of Josephine settled upon him like a shadow. I think, she had said the other day, her voice tight in all those miles of cable, I think maybe it's too much, these conversations while we're waiting. We just shouldn't talk until something happens. Anton looked at the phone, wondering what she really meant. I don't know, he said. The receiver in his hand with its little rubbery coiling cord seemed so slight, so tenuous. Well, all right, he'd finally said. We'll see.

He should not have started designing anything before making some headway with all the *uffizi*, but willfully, he had, wanting to show Signore Manin something exciting as soon as possible. But this afternoon, feeling ragged, he was halfway through the park before realizing he'd forgotten his documents and new drawings. He ran back, got the drawings, so missed the boat, and ended up walking most of the way.

Then, as he was hurrying through the passage to Signore Manin's, Anton saw a woman stepping from his door. Her eyes were hidden beneath a hat, but he had a quick glimpse of green-veined wrists as she pulled her coat close, and some sort of private conversation was still visible on her mouth, which seemed too full and live. She did not look at Anton when she passed, her heels hard on the paving stones, and he forced himself not to look at her as she disappeared down the passage. But all he could think was: *Others*.

"*Buona sera*," said Signore Manin, looking flustered at his door. "Wait—no—ah, too late. Vera left something behind." He told Anton to have a seat while he went into the next room, where Anton could see him fussily rolling a sheet of paper and tapping it into a tube.

So there we are, he thought.

Vera.

Argentinean? Spanish? The name seemed familiar. He'd read something recently, hadn't he, about Vera someone, a prize. Was it Vera? There hadn't been a picture. Was it in Barcelona? Madrid? And had he seen her somewhere? A jury?

But now Oswaldo was back, waiting to see his new drawings. At the very touch of them, the very sight of the Derwent and Prismacolor sketches, all thoughts of this Vera flew to the rim of Anton's skull. His hands trembled as he produced the first drawing, such a dramatic one, at night, wild blues and whites and blacks. He was smitten all over again, and even as he spoke, as he described and suggested, he could see the structure rising on the dark sea, see light transfusing his walls of water.

"Yes," murmured Oswaldo after he had adjusted his glasses

and studied the drawings. "Yes." Anton glanced up to see that Oswaldo's eyes had grown slightly misty.

He has dreamt it already floats there, Anton thought, smothering his smile as he neatened the drawings. So, Vera, do his eyes grow damp for your villa, too?

After they'd discussed some details of light and had argued, with civility but hard, over some details of height, they looked at each other, sated.

"I'll take you home," said Oswaldo. As Anton rolled up his drawings, Oswaldo went into the other room and returned with the plastic tube.

In the boat Oswaldo sang softly. He turned to Anton as they made the large round between the Lido and Sant'Elena and said, "I must tell you, I really must tell you, how pleased I am about all of this. How very, very pleased I am with what you and Vera have done so far."

Anton smiled politely, sick, and got himself out of the boat.

But then alone, walking back through the park, his footsteps beat the cruel words into the hardened mud. Vera. Vera who? Was he supposed to know? He ought to know. Someone important, someone with whom Signore Manin was very, very pleased. And he of course had no idea who she was; he was completely out of touch. It came from always drifting, he thought bitterly. No, it came from being marooned in New Orleans almost a year; how can you keep track of anything down there? All that swampy rot. He was grinding his jaw. Very pleased with what you both have done. Why tell him that? A sly little trick to push him on? Well, he was a tough old businessman, wasn't he? He knew how to do things.

That night, again the penguins waddled back and forth over the ribboning ramps. Josephine dove into their pool, which was no longer clear but green and oily, waving with ghostly weeds. Anton saw her swim up against the glass, her pink arms stretched behind, bubbles streaming from her nose, slim body arched, and mermaid tail swaying, dull silver, behind her. He woke from the dream distempered and sweating and burned his espresso pot on the stove, having forgotten the water.

Lach thought about it very hard but finally decided that there was no choice: his show was opening in two weeks, and he always felt better if he wore certain shoes. Besides, the season was changing, and he needed fresh clothes. He called Vera first, but she wasn't home, so he left a message; then she called and left her own, saying when he might come. It seemed that she planned to be there. Well, of course she did! Lach was nervous on the boat going over, excited to enter his sweet little house but imagining himself inside its walls all alone with Vera. And when was the last time? He could hardly remember. Last summer? Last summer! He shuddered. Imagine. His palms were slick as he got off the boat and bounded along the *fondamenta*; sunlight fell bright on the pink house. There was no doorbell, so he banged, feeling like the big bad wolf.

"Sorry," he said when Vera opened the door. She didn't answer, but with a nod allowed him to go up the stairs first. He was aware of her eyes on his back. The ground floor still smelled of brick scale and what might be moldering insects, but even this smell filled Lach with sad longing.

On the main floor she didn't offer him anything to drink or ask him to sit down, so after bouncing on his toes for a moment, he went about his business. She shadowed him, paces away, as he rummaged through drawers and closets; he moved through the few rooms fast. As he climbed the ladder to the bedroom loft, he felt her watching from below, and with a jerk of his head he kept the end of the striped scarf from tangling around his feet on the rungs. Upstairs, he was embarrassed to be treading the floor above her head, embarrassed to be near her things. He tried not to look at them, yet there was a faint scent of her everywhere, a smell he only now realized he'd forgotten. And while he fumbled around, it seemed to him that the ghost of Francesca watched from the bed. But was it even the ghost of Francesca? Or the ghost of Vera herself, lying just beneath it? Lach was confused a moment and blinked. The scarf about his neck was too tight. Let's hope, he thought, there won't be any *scenes*.

He skidded down the ladder, one arm draped with clothes. "Getting warmer," he said brightly, feeling his face hot and pink. He glanced around the room—*his* room!—distressed to see it so full of her work, and for an instant he imagined all her heavy rich pigments leaching back into his walls, suffusing them forever. All those layers of darkness, all her extravagant blues. Pavonazzo! He nearly said it—but what a *terrible* thing to do. Lach noticed then that her work was all studies of faces. No, he realized, just one face. One face vigorously studied. An old walrus face, with Tiepolo brows.

Good god, he thought. It's Manin.

Lach carefully did not catch her eye but moved his own eyes from one image of that old face to another, looking out judgmentally from his own walls.

A commission. But how did she get it?

Normally she did saints!

And Lach hadn't even been *asked*.

He turned with an effort, smiling broadly, as if to appear encouraging. Then he fished in his pocket and produced a card. "Here," he said.

"What?" She looked suspicious.

"My show. In two weeks. An invitation." He was frankly surprised at the sound of his voice.

She looked at the card but didn't take it. "I already have one."

"Of course. That's right. Of course you do." Well, she was on the mailing list; he'd only *thought* that one personally given . . . He felt hot and looked around again, arms muffled in clothing.

"Oswaldo Manin," he found himself saying, pointing with an elbow toward a sketch on the wall.

"Yes," she said. She did not go on.

"Portrait?" he said stupidly.

She nodded, eyes opaque.

So what could he do? He raised his brows, congratulatory. She was obviously not going to tell him a thing; he was certainly not going to ask her. He made a hapless farewell gesture beneath the heap of clothes and hurried outside, whistling.

Now Lucinde was away again, and Max had hardly even seen her since New Year's. Her pipes were all broken, she'd said, and she couldn't bear to be in the house without water, so she was running back to Biloxi until they were fixed. Thus time ambled on, and Max tried to cheer himself with the notion that the more time ambled along, the more it accumulated, and therefore accumulated on his side, proving the depths of his patience. It was true, furthermore, that she did not do altogether nothing; she sent him sweet little notes, for instance, which he rolled up and tucked into pilsner glasses and displayed on a shelf. Sweet notes, sighing notes: So much work! she lamented. So little money, so little time! She was hunting a location near Pass Christian for a film based on a book he hadn't heard of, a film she sounded pleased about; he'd had the impression of white muslin and heat.

This evening Max took the newest card she'd sent, a collage of quotations (he gathered) from that unknown book, together with a drink out to the balcony, where he sat wrapped up in a blanket. Thank heavens the pipes in his house hadn't frozen; the grim typist out back declared it was the warmth of the termites that had saved them, all that motion and metabolism going on inside the walls. Max looked down at the planks of his balcony and kicked his heel against one; it *seemed* solid enough. He took a sip and then a swallow of his drink and gazed down chilly Rue Royale toward the imagined house on Esplanade.

But it wasn't imagined: cards came from there or from wherever she went, Biloxi or Pass Christian, as she was drawn over the misty bayous by a team of pelicans or however it was she traveled. She sent her cards, and she made phone calls, his answering machine breathing forth that extraordinary voice that fell all over him, besotting. Max held up the latest card in the fading light, pressed its sharp corner to the roots of his hair, and drew a line down his forehead. When it reached the bridge of his nose, he shut his left eye so he saw only to the right up Rue Royale, then his right eye so he saw only to the left. Toward her, away from her. Or not quite her, that hallowed space. He shut both eyes.

Max, Max, Max, was what she said. You know, I just don't *know*, is all. But please don't be disheartened.

Well, this was simply his project. A sailor following the north star, and why not? He would follow it until he could follow no longer. The north star? Or the morning star, the evening star; no star at all but a wandering planet, traveling her own silent path.

Max looked down at himself in the dusky light, at his rumpled new trousers protruding from the blanket.

When Therese had stood at the door that day and seen him sitting there, her eyes slowly filled with tears, and he did not know what to say. He sat there, blinking, his mouth in that shape. Then he'd gotten up, hurried past her, gone out into the obliterating wind.

The sky was dark now, the last light gone. He looked into the dim ballroom, where the tea chests stood like rocks in the sea, most of them still unopened. He swallowed the last of his drink. He really ought to unpack. A crowbar, a knife. He went to the kitchen and opened a drawer and looked into it, but slowly shut it again and poured another drink. Such a sense of travel, he felt then, the floor creaking under his feet, she in the air behind the pelicans' beating wings. Yet surely she'd have to settle. Sometime?

In the darkness Max's eyes fell upon his battered briefcase. He snapped it open, emptied out all the papers and uncapped pens, and brushed and blew the briefcase clean. Certainly there was room enough. A bottle, plus two of the best glasses. Ice?

And it should be somewhere safe. A neutral ground?

The levee.

Fine, thought Josephine, as she stood in a bathroom stall at work and stared into her underpants. She pulled them down and tried to step out of them but became tangled and lost her balance, eyes stinging. Finally she got them off and stuffed them into the waste bin. In the toilet a bright drop of blood blossomed like an anemone, the delicate red edges thinning.

All the pipes were fixed now. Everything was fixed. Everything was back to normal. She stood still in the stall, looking down at her shoes and at the scrap of tampon wrapper that had drifted to the floor.

I told you, I told you, I told you. There is no reason to hope.

She flushed. Off to the Sargasso Sea, she thought. Go play with your brothers and sisters.

The water spun, gurgled, and rushed away, into the bayous, the sea.

After work Josephine walked along Saint Charles directly to the K&B. The palm trees were still blackened from the freeze, the oleanders withered.

As she stood at the counter with her box of Tampax and aspirin and a pair of nice dark bottles, she felt the eyes of the cashier upon her. She looked up; he promptly looked down at his machine. He had pickled skin and hair bleached white and a ring in his reddened nose. Sometimes he worked in the back; was that him? At the pharmacist's counter? He looked up again through a hanging lock of hair. Yes, him, sometimes he was back there, certainly that was him, in a white smock or shirt, whatever it was they wore. Like Doctor Gare's. He knew her name. Everything she bought. He knew all sorts of things. Josephine got confused a moment, the cash register becoming a computer. He stared at it again. Did they talk? Pharmacists, doctors, all the others? He was ringing up the bottles, lifting each to find its price, and heat began to burn through her skin.

I'm just taking a break, she thought to him hard.

So it doesn't matter what I do.

All right?

It just does not matter what I do!

"Well!" cried someone.

She spun around. That man with his strangely lined face and pale, waving hair stood behind her in line, that Max, his own arms full of bottles.

"Cheers," he said, and lifted one, and toasted the air before her, jolly.

When Lucinde reached the levee, Max was already standing there, beaming, having obviously run to get there first because he was so often late. They walked a short way and sat on a bench that faced the river, and then he opened his briefcase with a flourish, and she saw that it was packed with ice. Festively he produced frosted glasses and a bottle, pried the cork free, and poured. They sipped from their bubbling glasses, the briefcase balanced on his lap, and Lucinde noticed that it dripped from a corner, forming a little dark pit by his foot. He seemed to have cut his hair and to have on a new shirt, and the bright chartreuse collar was so stiff that again one wing flipped up, grazing his chin as he talked, although he did not seem to notice. Perhaps because he was holding her hand.

Max held it lightly and as one usually holds not a hand but a tray of canapés, balancing it upon his open palm with his thumb curving over to keep it in place. Lucinde had decided to let her hand rest there a time, but as it did, she could feel all the quick heat and light that ran through her body gathering there, and she could tell that as Max slid his own palm back and forth beneath hers, secretly he was measuring, gauging, as if to discover whether fateful new lines had appeared. She was counting the seconds that she had not altogether consciously allotted for this moment, seeing the tiny grains fall through the narrow glass waist.

She held up her glass to the lowering sun.

"When you drop a sugar cube into champagne," she asked, "what is it that happens?"

"I believe it bubbles."

"Just bubbles?"

No fish were jumping from the river, too late.

"Someone says that it is marvelous, no, *meraviglioso*," she went on, "the way you can drop a sugar cube into coffee and it dissolves, but when you drop your own self into the bath you don't." It was simply so hard to fathom, that she, herself, her senses and thoughts, were held inside a thin, stretchy skin and that everything outside was different, not she.

Max seemed to be pondering this, squinting out over the river. Lucinde allowed herself to look at him, really look at him, her eyes traveling so close along those unusual lines that she almost could feel them, feel the softness of his blond brows.

But then he turned to her, his eyes surprisingly close. "They grew sugarcane here, no?"

Lucinde paused a second before nodding, registering a sliver of despair. She made herself try again. "But don't you think it's interesting?" she said. "I mean, that business about skin?"

He blinked, and she thought she detected his fingers tensing.

She shut her eyes. "Here I am in mine. There you are in your own. And outside it, everything's foreign."

"Yes," he answered, one knee jogging.

"Do you know what I mean?" she asked. "That one really just can't get out?" But as she looked at him, she thought, No. She looked at her own hand lying upon his. It seemed to be burning; she withdrew it.

"You see," she began, her hand safely back in her lap. She

paused, smiled graciously, made an enormous effort. "You see, Maximus, I seem to have trouble."

"Trouble?"

The Algiers ferry was just beginning its turn in the middle of the river, in the strongest current, the turn that never seemed possible.

"Trouble?" Max said again. He leaned toward her, those watery blue eyes concerned.

"Excuse me?" Lucinde was startled by his sudden proximity.

"You said," he said.

She looked at her watch. "Oh god, I'm late," she said, rising quickly. "Sorry. Got to go."

The next time they met, that woman was actually in Signore Manin's boat, sitting behind him like Cleopatra. As Anton climbed down the slick embankment stones, clutching his rolls and black book, her eyes seemed to follow his awkward legs. Oswaldo turned to nod at Anton and made a gesture of introduction, but only the name Vera was audible, the rest lost in the wind and the growl of the motor. As if Anton hadn't known that much already! As if it weren't a thorn in his brain. She looked at him and nodded. Then she murmured something, and it actually sounded like Palladio.

Anton's cheeks flooded with heat, but he nodded back stiffly from his side of the boat and made a despairing gesture about not being able to hear over the engine. He stared intently into the lagoon until Oswaldo stopped again by the Redentore and helped her out of the boat. But then she said it again: "Pleasure, Palladio." With a quick little smile. Anton's face went rigid.

Then, throughout their meeting at Oswaldo's house, as Anton showed him the newest drawings, Oswaldo seemed distracted. He looked down at the perspectives and plans, the wonderful organic shapes, the watery walls, the rivulet Anton had planned down the middle, and then his gaze wandered off. Oswaldo had not even said her last name. At one point he pushed a paper away and simply looked down at the table's surface, so that Anton did the same, staring wretchedly at the slab's sandlike strata and pale vitreous bands.

"Onyx," said Oswaldo after a time. "From the Greek for nail, or claw. I cannot recall why." He considered his nails, then gazed again at the table. "Something liquid even about *stone*," he said, "isn't there?" He looked up, unseeing, and Anton suddenly noticed how old the man was.

That evening Anton sat at his desk, staring at ripped sheets of trace, photographs, broken leads, a protractor stabbed into a wad of eraser, a few torn pieces of mail.

His blood had gone still when Josephine finally told him. Each time he felt it like falling, something beneath him falling away.

He put a cold hand to his forehead. Inside him, on the floor of his stomach, her ring rusted.

Max.

No. Oh no. That got him nowhere. He would not even let the thought surface.

Anton drummed his fingers on the desk. He looked at his drawing. He had been thinking about oolitic limestone, how to imprint a pattern like that, sea snails and worms and fragments of shells, into the concrete of his slabs. He'd much prefer using that limestone itself, but it was probably too expensive.

What was *Palladio* supposed to mean?

Was it her name for him, or Oswaldo's? Certainly Oswaldo did not call her anything other than her own name, respectful. Anton's knee jogged as he returned to his drawing; his bare feet on the floor were cold. He stopped, pulled one up, and massaged it. Studying the drawing before him, he began to rub the blue eraser on the dirty ball of his foot and looked down with disgust.

Palladio. It could not be anything but mockery. But what had he done? He looked around at his drawings, the ones on the Mayline, the ones taped to the wall. There was nothing Palladio about them. Modern, beautiful, far more Minoletti or Nervi than Palladio.

Or was that the problem? Were his drawings too modern? Irony. Was it irony? But why otherwise would the man have hired him? He'd seen Anton's work; he'd read his articles; surely he knew what he was getting.

But oh no, god, no—suddenly it became clear. Could Anton be a dummy, a *ringer*?

Why? There was no committee and no need for a ringer unless there was a committee to manipulate. Or in fact was there one? Of which Anton knew nothing? Someone else who had to be tricked into choosing the right design, Vera's design, by virtue of the contrast?

A wife? Was there a wife?

A wife. Anton looked down at his empty hands, at his drawings. Drawing after drawing was all he did, drawings and words, papery stuff, words and futile gestures, things floating into the darkness. Nothing was ever solid. He could make nothing solid. He would sweat and labor and then disappear, without leaving a single trace.

He placed both feet on the cold floor.

He looked at the telephone for a moment. But he didn't move. He looked again at his drawings, his desk. Then his eyes fell upon a piece of mail he'd received by mistake, a postcard sent to the apartment's owner. It had an image of rubble or something, shells, bottles, trash. He turned it over. An opening. It would be on the Giudecca, in a boathouse. Anton rubbed his eyes, weary. How could it be that he hadn't even photographed a boathouse yet, after all this time in Venice? The most obvious type of water architecture, and he had not documented a single one.

Because Lach always had little fights with the *curatrice* about how things were to be displayed—but this time, really, he had to have his own way—he went there a week before the show to make sure everything was right. Placement: his arrangements had to follow the island's contours exactly; they had to be just as he'd found the objects themselves. As he rode the boat over the lagoon, gripping the gunnel with one chapped hand, Lach admitted to himself that he was just a little anxious. Anxious, after all these years and all these shows! Well sure, why not? It was a sign of health.

He got off the boat and clanked over the walkway to the square beside his little pink house. There, in full view, he stopped to light a cigarette, without even looking up. Would she come to the opening? Who knew? He was surprised he even wondered. He walked along the *fondamenta* and took a left, made one or two turns through ruined buildings and then alleys of beached boats, until he reached the southern edge of the island, his boathouse, the slip.

Lach walked down the slip and stood there awhile, his shoes partly in the water. Little waves lapped; the air was cool and smelled fishy, of salt; across the water lay a few small islands, floating in the haze. It was real sea here, real island, real mud;

funny how easily you'd forget it. What a perfect place for his show. *Liminal*, he thought: one of those words like *pavonazzo*, or like *fata morgana*, words that sounded so im*press*ive. Yes, it was liminal, here where he stood; at the very juncture between all those heaps of culture—he poked at the air behind him with his elbow—and all this thoughtless sea.

All right, all right, all *right*, thought Josephine. She opened the dresser drawer, pulled out the white box, and took from it a needle, a syringe, and a handful of vials. She went to the bathroom, sat on the tub, and stared at the things in her hands. There is no reason not to do this again, there is no reason not to try, not to hope, because hope should spring eternal, shouldn't it? And look, it's nearly spring.

In Mrs. Mouton's garden next door things were coming back to life: rosebuds opening, crepe myrtle blooming in big soft tufts of pink, jasmine and bougainvillaea climbing. So obliging the way this happened. Still, so easy to see ahead, to see those soft blossoms wither and fall and have to go through all this business once more. The palm trees remained black.

She snapped off the top of a glass vial and poked the needle into the liquid. Next door Mrs. Mouton came out to her garden with a cup of coffee and a roll, which she chewed gingerly, as if aware of her teeth. Josephine drew the liquid into the syringe, squirted it into the next vial, and stirred to dissolve the tiny white ball, to make the potion that would soon be inside her.

There was an old woman who swallowed a spider.

Picture it tumbling in the darkness, confused. Now, if it were a water spider—

The telephone rang. She didn't move. She stared down the hall and waited. Seven rings, eight rings, nine, ten; he always stopped at ten. Then it was quiet, the last ring dissolving inside the walls. Josephine looked at the walls, all full of those ghostly rings. It had comforted Anton that in fact they were plaster, not Sheetrock, as in newer houses; he had knocked with his knuckles, pleased at the sound, not knowing that the rare termites infesting New Orleans ate plaster as well as wood, not to mention live oak roots and sugarcane. She knew all about this now because of the latest proposal, to fund research into how best to kill them before they devoured the Quarter. In any one of these walls might be a channel of insects, heads enlarged, mandibles working, consuming the house from inside. She had begun studying the walls, touching what looked like cracks but turned out to be dry rivers, the negative trails left behind by the termites. If she ran her finger along one, the crust of paint would give way, and behind it the wall was hollow.

She looked down again at the syringe, the needle, the little glass egg. Then she drew up the liquid, held the needle to the sun, and pressed until a drop appeared at the tip. She pressed a little harder, until the drop became large and burst and spilled, a shower as delicate as pins and needles on her hand. She looked down at her stomach, pinched the skin, and held the needle close.

If only this syringe had the thing itself in it, and this business could all be done.

If only a little homunculus.

Because what if the walls of the house became empty, and she was empty, too?

Oswaldo told himself firmly that everything was proceeding well. He jingled the coins and the pumice stone in his pocket and assured himself that really he could not imagine being more pleased with the building his Palladio was designing or the painting Vera had begun. His villa would float like a shell, light and transparent yet defying—defying!—the violent sea that raged all around it, and he himself would be portrayed within, ancient and modern, enduring. He was pleased. Of course he was pleased.

But still—

Oswaldo looked around at a litter of drawings: sketches and symbolical diagrams of himself and his things that Vera had torn from her pad and let drift; details of his villa that Anton had pushed across the table with a shaking hand, bidding him make decisions. Oswaldo's glasses rested at the end of his nose, tickling and uncomfortable. He took them off and rubbed his eyes and caught a blurred glimpse of himself in the mirror; his lower eyelids sagged, reddened like a mastiff's. Whatever are you doing? he thought. Because again, despite how pleased he surely should be, it was creeping in: that worm of panic.

He pushed away all the drawings and went to his bed and sat. Looking at his crimson coverlet, he laid his wrinkled hand upon it. Crimson that was once so valuable now had become so cheap, synthetic. This sort of thing dismayed him. Even a substance like pepper had been greatly valued once; it had been used as currency, carefully locked up. A pound of pepper, or ginger, or cinnamon: they were wealth itself, enough to fend off the taxman for months! Now all of it was worth almost nothing. How did this happen? How did things that once seemed so valuable become utterly worthless? Things once worth their weight in gold were now packaged in plastic bottles. It was all so shifty, so brief.

The panic began to take quiet hold of his chest. He stood and made himself resume his work, picking up another of Vera's images to see what in it he liked. Lots of blues, she used so many blues, but imagine if any were still made of lapis lazuli! Ultramarine, so precious it took its name from the vast distance it traveled, far beyond the sea; so precious that paintings were even judged by its presence. Yet even that did not last. Genuine or not, so many pigments were fugitive and grew sooty or gray. With an effort he lifted another image and held the two side by side upon the wall to consider them, to see which had him as he would like to be remembered.

But then, as his fingertips held the papers to the cold, damp wall, he could not help but think how water seeped through the floors of museums and churches, through the foundations and then through the tiles. The marble itself seemed as porous as charcoal and drew the liquid up. Moisture rose first through the old, cracked floors, up inside the inlaid walls, then crept into the gilt frames of the paintings, and seeped into the gorgeous canvases themselves. Gradually paint that had been so artfully laid would lift away from the canvas; moist blisters of pigment would pucker and split; then paint would hang in loose scales. And every so often a scale would fall, so that a little pile of flakes gradually gathered upon the tiles of the floor, like graceful stalagmites of pigment. And what the water didn't do the air surely would: gassy air drifting over from Mestre, air that gnawed on marble and paint, air dense with the fumes of ancient carbonized fossils, themselves the traces of creatures long since turned back into earth.

He looked at the pictures. He tried to breathe.

A hundred years at the most.

Max sat in his ballroom with a row of books open on the long table, investigating the history of carnival. His starting point had been the king cakes and his happy surprise at biting down on a little plastic figurine, but of course that was a familiar phenomenon—much like the silver trinkets in old Christmas puddings or even the surprise in the Cracker Jack box. Suggesting fertility and so on, he suspected, but also possibility, luck, and chance? *Anyone* might get it, after all; everything was fair! He'd already taken down a few notes on the concept of carnival: *first pagan (Osiris, Dionysus, etc.), then Christian. Fertility, springtime, resurrection. Suspension of order, dissolution, misrule. Out with the old and in with the new!* One small discovery particularly pleased him: that carnival did not mean *farewell to flesh*, as he'd always worried, but instead *to lighten flesh*. To relieve it, he now saw; to comfort, console.

Max looked up from his book and pondered this. To console? For what? But now the business about king cakes became even more clear: *certainly* an expression of fertility, as was the throwing of plastic beads. *Like seeds!* he wrote. *Confetti, rice!* He knew a little about the parades and floats but then wondered why exactly they were called floats. After hunting awhile, he discovered, with great cheer, a note about the very first float, when Dionysus proceeded from the sea in a wheeled ship streaming ivy and music and wine (after he'd gotten away from the kidnapping pirates—and imagine pirates kidnapping a god—by turning their shackles into vines and the pirates themselves into dolphins). Max had even found a picture of a beautiful ancient wine bowl, upon whose bottom the story was depicted, and he gazed at this longingly, imagining the bowl on his mantelpiece: the crescent-shaped ship, the bunches of grapes dangling, the slender, leaping dolphins.

After a while he decided that all this was reason enough to ring Lucinde.

"I'll take you to all the right parades," she assured him. "You can skip the trashy ones."

He told her the business about lightening flesh.

"*Light*ning flesh?" she said. "Thunder?"

"No, no, *light*ening, *light*ening flesh. To make light of it," he said. "Consolation."

"Consolation," she repeated. She seemed to think about the word.

"Although I'm not certain for what," he said brightly.

"No?" she replied. She laughed. "But don't worry," she went on, "I'll manage you during all the parades. Comus, Bacchus, Zulu, Rex."

He took a moment to write down the names and the dates. He drew balloons around *pagan* and *Christian*.

"But by the way, Maxwell," Lucinde said then, "as we're speaking of such things, there's something I've been wondering about. Tell me, do you happen to have any faith?"

Max looked out the balcony door, uneasy, and shifted his position on the uneven chair. "Faith?" he said. "In what?"

"Oh, I suppose I mean religious faith. Belief or some such, I guess."

"Ah," he said. "No, I don't think so. Do I? I'm not quite sure I do."

"I see," she said.

There was a silence. Max watched a large bubble from the boy downstairs rise slowly by the balcony railing. It wobbled, iridescent.

"Do you?" he said then.

She sighed. "I don't think so. Although I expect it's a comfort. If one has it."

"Indeed, so do I," he replied promptly. "At least, I suspect." Max did not know what to say and put his feet neatly together as he smoothed the spine of a book, wondering how to retreat from this particular branch of the conversation. He would like to go back to the parades and floats.

"Really"—Lucinde was continuing, a little singsong now— "faith in *any*thing would be fine."

The bubble was clinging to the rail, one end of it gently pulled by the breeze. It wavered, grew.

"But such a leap." She sighed.

Max thought inconsequentially of a leap from the balcony and sat up now, concerned. "Leap?"

"Excuse me?"

The bubble stretched and suddenly popped.

"Yes, leap!" he cried then, understanding, standing up, books tumbling to the floor.

"Just like *that*?" she said with her wonderful drawl. She laughed, although he thought he could just hear the edge of her laugh pull away.

He panicked, staring down Royale to her invisible house. "Let's meet," he said. "Now. Let's meet at Napoleon's."

"All right," she said. "No. I don't think so. I don't know. Napoleon's? By the way, did you ever call her?"

"Who?"

"That woman. That Josephine. That funny little lush, with the ring."

He sat down. "Was she?"

"What?"

"A lush?"

"Lush, lush," Lucinde said, and he could imagine her eyes shut, her tongue lingering on the roof of her mouth. "It's a wonderful word, you know, *lush* . . ."

"Yes?"

"Lush, luscious, luxuriant . . . a lush with rich, curling red hair . . ."

Now she was laughing again, this time with no shrinking away but throaty and just a little bit wild. Max found himself putting his hand to his neck.

It was cold the night of Lach's opening, but as people filled the boathouse, the air became gaseous with wine and seemed like a fog of warm light. Everything seemed to be in order again, Lach thought happily: he had on his favorite old shoes, he was having a show. And not just a show, a show in Venice. He stood near the entrance, his back to the sea, his sailor-striped shirt on under his sweater. He'd had shows in New York and London but never in Venice, which he knew was hardly the same sort of scene, but all the same it pleased him. He ran a stubby finger around the glass in his hand, looking at all the people.

There were rich old men with silver hair atop polished brows, wearing silk ties in Bellini colors; there were dowagers with gray coiffures in tailored black chiffon, their dark eyes lined with kohl, discerning. That pair of blond Venetians he always saw on the *passeggiata* had come, a brother and sister, so handsome that whenever he saw them all he could think was the word *nobility*. Everyone moved over and around his little arrangements of shells and barnacles and trash, no idea at all that they themselves were now part of the patterns of things found on beaches and pilings, natural agglomerations. So comforting! Lach thought. These collections of like. Because that's all it really *is*, he thought. People like to be to*ge*ther.

He sighed contentedly, took a drink of wine, and wished that he could suddenly jump like Pan and fly way up and look down at all of this, these amazing islands glinting on the black water. All of this city with its precious minerals and slabs of stone and downright human *brilliance*. And here Lach was, part of it, in his sailor-striped shirt and favorite shoes, his lank blond hair disheveled. He shut his eyes and let himself think it: the line runs straight from Vivarini to me. And soon I'll be back in my little pink house! A coin seemed to drop inside him, lighting everything up.

A waiter passed by, and Lach got rid of his old glass and took a new one; then, humming, he moved along the edge of the crowd. There was Manin, across the room, gazing down at the plastic bottles. Of course Manin had come; all that business about not being asked to do his portrait just didn't mean a thing now, did it? Between Lach and the Fondazione there'd been a kind of patronage for nearly a decade now! The old man lifted his gaze from the bottles, and Lach raised his glass to him from across the room; Manin peered nearsightedly back, then nodded—nodded in a manner that Lach decided was *profound*. The old man of the sea, easy to picture him rising up with a triton; something to do with his moustache. Lach hummed again and moved along, skirting the room so as not actually to intrude upon the patterns being unwittingly made by all these splendid people. But he should have had mirrors installed in the ceiling; he should have rigged up some cameras! For a moment Lach was crushed by the oversight, but then he realized, no, of course not, the point was the ephemerality, wasn't it? Tides and so on. There was Vera. What on earth was she wearing? For some reason she held her emptied glass behind her, trailing it upside down like a tail. Oh dear, he thought, overcome with tenderness: a little girl in the great big woods, leaving drops so that she'll find her way home again. Maybe he'd just go talk to her. Poor thing, all alone. And anyway, Francesca—

He did not actually want to think about Francesca. He did not see how the problem at her aunt's house in Tuscany could really require her to be away just now.

When he looked back, Vera had disappeared—no, there she was, talking to Manin. And why not? No doubt they were close. Her head was bowed a little, that submissive sacrificial thing she did, or at least it seemed submissive, but he wasn't likely to soon forget that crack in the New York wall, now was he?

Just then she and Manin turned their heads and stared directly at him. They did not just stare at him; they fixed him with a look that seemed to drive through him, and Lach stood, shocked, as if speared.

But as he stood there, pierced by eyes, he had a sudden vision. The very scene he himself was part of seemed to him all at once like a painting, one of those glorious big church paintings, in which the composition and all the motion are helped along by the glances: patron to saints, and saints to Madonna, and Madonna down to the child, who was the center of everything, in a halo of rays.

Lach giggled nervously, fixed. Well, no wonder, he thought. No wonder I wasn't even asked about the portrait: of course Vera told Manin everything! Just as she and that Lucinde were plotting, just as she wept to all her friends in New York. All right, he thought. I'm sorry! He swallowed more wine. But I couldn't *help* it! he thought. Things change.

Something made Lach turn. He wasn't sure what, an obscure little tugging. He turned his head quickly and saw that behind him, coming in, was that dark fellow of the Redentore. And it was at him, in fact, not Lach at all, that Manin and Vera were gazing.

Lach moved quickly away and resumed humming. He patted at his bottom for cigarettes.

Francesca hadn't even *called*.

It was maybe just a bit too warm here; there were maybe too many people. Suddenly Lach stumbled and found he was standing within one of his arrangements. In his surprise he stepped back, awkwardly, with no grace at all.

Anton made an effort to look at the show, at what seemed to him to be piles of trash but which no doubt were much, much more. He took a glass of wine, had a failed conversation, and retreated, reddened, to a wall. This boathouse didn't even offer him much. It was completely on land, and all redone, only the slip of any interest, and little. The fact that he had come to an opening of someone he didn't know from sheer panic—that he had even crashed it—indicated how badly he was spiraling.

There was Signore Manin, across the room. Anton smiled quickly, made a little nodding bow. He had never really managed to call him Oswaldo, and after that first time he had not been corrected, which of course meant something. Manin was talking to—no need to look. That inky head, one hand at the moment behind her own back, finger and thumb secretly designing.

Anton found he was almost crushing the fragile flute of his glass, and for a moment he wanted to do just that, snap it, grind the glass back into the sand it was made of. He controlled himself, relaxed his grip, ran a thumb up and down the stem. Glass, in vitro. Now Josephine was going through that horror again. And of course she had to. She'd said it between her teeth: the *insurance*. So as soon as it seemed that something was happening, that his contribution, as Doctor Gare put it, was required, he would have to be ready to fly home. He'd have to start looking into a ticket tomorrow.

Fly home, and then what? Come back?

Anton took a sip of wine and shut his eyes. All around him were Venetians, people who seemed to have slipped from the city's paintings or emerged from the depths of the marble floors; people who seemed made of a rare substance, to be suffused with the very richness and texture of the city, its value. It was in this room all around him; he had never been closer, he was painfully close. He would never come closer at all.

Vera turned her head away from Manin just then, smiling, her dark eyes brushing Anton's face.

That was it. He put his glass down on something he guessed was not a piece and left. Outside, in the darkness, the air was cold and damp; the sea gently lapped. A few lights glimmered across the lagoon, but the water was black, black. Anton walked down the slip to the water's edge. Real sea here, sloshing, real mud. He took a breath, shut his eyes. You could actually forget all about that culture behind you; it could slide down this ramp, underwater. And one day of course it would. The sea stretched before him, a few shapes of islands black against the sky. He let a little water creep around his shoe and watched the ripples, the faint lines of light.

He had stood at the window a long time, looking down at the floating white arms, the floating striped tie, imagining his father could really hold his breath for so long, counting each of the seconds.

Anton turned and walked quickly away, through the empty boatyards and ruins to the *fondamenta*. He waited by the Redentore awhile, looking at the city's flickering skyline and up at the glowing church, then he took a vaporetto to the Zattere. There he walked not to the Accademia but along the dark embankment to the Dogana, the Salute, and stood there on the point. His throat was tight and dry as he looked at San Giorgio, the far glimmer of the Lido. Soon it would all have been a dream, and he would leave, return to—what?

Long black boats nudged each other, creaking; water slapped against the embankment. The last *traghetto* was about to cross, and the oarsman looked at him, questioning. He stepped in. As they glided through the water, Anton made himself stand. The dark sea jostled, level with his knees, held off by the floating black shell.

By late February it was already spring in New Orleans, and Lucinde was spring-cleaning; she liked to sluice out the house. What she would really like to do was take fine white plaster of Paris and line the walls, thicken them, or not even plaster of Paris but porcelain, something hard and gleaming and white. She filled a bucket with water and soap, poured it on the bleached wooden floor, got down on her knees, and scrubbed. A nice sound, the rough swish of the brush, her hands pink among the bubbles. She had not bothered putting on clothes.

Maybe, she had been thinking, maybe—

I've been thinking, she would say to Max, that maybe, perhaps, you might just be right.

Oh? he would say, and she would hear his short breath, hear him sit down, perhaps even hear a nervous jingling of ice.

Yes, she'd go on, it might just be better to dive right in. That's what you say, isn't it? Just go ahead and make the leap?

Lucinde stood up, stood still, and tried to imagine it. Leap in, or leap *out*? She swayed on the wet floor, her hands dripping at either side. It was such a simple thing, such a thoughtless thing, a thing that should not be thought about, like breathing. So very simple: just make the leap.

It was awfully hot. She looked down at herself, and it seemed a longer way down than usual. Perhaps because of the shining floor, space unfolding in that direction, too. It was *awfully* hot; Lucinde turned on the air conditioner and stood a moment before the cool draft, watching the water and sweat dry upon her arm, leaving the fine blond hairs bleached. She thought of something she'd recently heard, about a woman in Metairie; it seemed that she had closed herself inside her apartment and turned the air-conditioning all the way up. Apparently she was in there a very long time, never went out, took nothing in. So at some point or other she'd died, but she hadn't starved; she'd dehydrated. When they found her, she was mummified, neat and dry, on her bed.

Lucinde went back to her bucket and refilled it. How would that feel, to mummify? Had she even been under sheets and blankets? Or had she wanted that cold air to fall pure upon her, upon her arms and throat and legs?

Lucinde touched her own throat, looked at her wet hand. Egyptian mummies, Max had said, were preserved in spices, in cumin, marjoram, and anise. It seemed very peaceful. Fragrant, and private. She wondered just how all this drying would look and considered her arms. Certainly not as they looked right now, all pink and plump. No, papery, thin, tight, much better. The bone would be articulated. Much, much better that way, she decided. She really did not see much use in all that excess flesh. But then again, she didn't like the idea of pure bone either; skeletons had a lack of individuality that she found disturbing. Just, yes, a hardening, a refining of the flesh. As when all that garish paint was finally worn off the ancient statues, and they were left bleached and clean.

Lucinde stood up and looked down at herself, then at herself reflected in the gleaming wet floors.

But what had she been thinking about earlier?

Josephine climbed up on Doctor Gare's table once more, the third time in the past six days. She dropped her legs over the bolsters, lay back, and tucked both hands behind her head. There was no more picture of Hawaii on the ceiling; instead, a poster of the Alps.

Doctor Gare was pleased that she noticed. "Nice to have a change, don't you think?" he said. "Hawaii in the winter, Alps in the summer. Relax, now, Josephine, please."

He slid in the instrument and studied the screen. First he maneuvered the thing to the left inside her, then he steered it hard to the right, and then back again to the left, but deeper; she pressed her fingertips to her eyes. But then he did it all again, revolving the instrument very slowly, so deep it seemed to scour. At last she felt the device go still. Doctor Gare cleared his throat, glanced at her, and blinked.

"So?" she said, up on her elbows.

He didn't answer, pulled the thing out, and peeled away the prophylactic.

"So?" she said again. "Just one?"

How, Lach wondered, do these things happen?

After his shows, it was true, he always felt funny. But today he was completely different. He hardly recognized himself! As if he'd woken up to find his old skin shed and wrinkled on the floor by the bed.

What had he *done?* he wondered, lying spread-eagled and naked after Francesca had gone to work. The watery light fell in between the long green shutters, the clatter of heels and delivery-men coming in from the *calle*. Where was he, and what on earth was he doing?

What I have done, Lach said as he stood up, is made an awful, *awful* mistake.

He moved around Francesca's apartment, picking up his things. Shoes, socks, books, a magazine. How was it that Francesca had looked so different the day before yesterday, when she came back from her aunt's? Tinny, or something, a little too tanned. And was her hair actually dyed? How could he never have noticed before? He glanced through the magazine and thought about hair dye; he thought about *capelli file d'oro*, the dye that Titian's cousin had developed when the blondes in the paintings became the rage, those blondes with their dark almond eyes.

And Francesca's lashes, too: there was something funny about them. Or maybe it was just how she looked at him? He almost hadn't recognized her! He glanced at an ad, a few reviews, and then riffled quickly to the listings. His show was mentioned in this issue: good. He always looked for his name in the listings and then scanned the other names nearby, to keep track of where he stood. And there was Vera, in the next column, because of her fellowship, plus the commission.

Lach pondered her name, the shape of its letters. He did not understand this. It suddenly seemed *new*.

He walked over the dusty tiles, putting things in a box. His espresso maker, his favorite little cups, all the scarves he'd left lying on chairs. Underwear, sweaters, a bag of old paint tubes.

Yes, he had always felt funny after his shows. Emptied or something.

So what else could he do?

Later, as he dialed the familiar number, he found that in the past few months it had become nearly exotic.

"Pronto?" said Vera, her voice hoarse.

"Hello," he said, suddenly nervous.

"Who is it?"

"Lach."

She did not say a thing, so he decided to go on. "Vera?"

"What?"

"I want to see you."

"Oh?"

"To talk."

She paused a moment. "Talk?"

"Yes."

She paused again. "About?"

He exhaled slowly. "Can I?"

"All right," she said. "Here?"

Somehow . . . "No," he said, and named a bar and a time. Before hanging up he gave her the phone number.

"For the place?" she asked.

"No, for me."

She was silent. Nearly giggling, he pictured her perplexed dark brows.

"'You'?" she said finally.

"What?"

"Just you?"

He touched a finger to the wall beside him and drew a long line like a crack. "Yes," he said, "just me." And he was shocked simply hearing the words. Had it ever been just him before?

"Oh," she said, and he squinted, casting himself through the phone to see if he could hear anything in her tone, see if he heard possibility.

Oswaldo could not sleep but lay stiff in his bed; since the earliest hours he'd sensed something in the air, a pressure or a pull. At last he opened his eyes and gave up. He got out of bed and threw his old robe over his shoulders and looked out the window. The tide. Of course it was the tide. One of the lowest he had ever seen. He dressed, put on his rubber boots, and went out.

It was a clear morning, the light not the hazy light that was so famous but crisp instead, more real. A little too sharp, mocking, even—it almost had a wickedness. And a tide this low, it was as if the elements had conspired, as if they were bent on making him see.

Oswaldo drove the boat slowly through the canal, then out and past the *fondamenta*, where deliverymen were tossing empty crates to boats. He had to bear left away from the island of San Michele, past Murano, and then head north toward the airport and terra firma; he had to follow the narrow canal with care. But he knew exactly where to go, and it was somewhere he did not want to go, because he knew he would see what he did not want to see. One saw it only at extremely low tides.

He moved forward, cautious, the water dangerously shallow, until he was as close as he could get. He secured the boat and, old legs aching, climbed out. The air smelled strong; nearby a heron stood knee-deep and blinked at him, then stretched out its wings and lumbered into the air. Oswaldo splashed through the water, mud sucking at his boots. Then at last he reached it.

Through just a few inches of brackish water he could make it out: fine ancient bricks in a herringbone pattern, clear water lapping over them gently. It was the floor of a villa two thousand years old.

Oswaldo gazed down at the ancient floor, at the rippling water.

Of course he accomplished nothing with his monuments, his mementi. Only a handful of sand thrown into the sea.

The preposterousness of a portrait. A villa!

Vanitas, he thought.

Why bother?

Suddenly he was exhausted. He longed for rest, the rest of stones. No, not even of stones, because they melted, they hardened, they exploded and flew. Not the rest of stones, then. The rest of night, the rest of the deepest, coldest night, the deepest, coldest ocean.

When Anton answered the phone, no one spoke at first.

"Josephine?" he said, hopefully, to the silence.

"Excuse me," said Signore Manin then, coughing, clearing his throat. "So sorry," he said. "But we'll have to put off our meeting."

"Of course, quite all right," said Anton, embarrassed. He fumbled in his book. "Tomorrow you might feel better? Or Wednesday?"

Oswaldo became vague. "No, no," he said. "I'm perfectly well. Not tomorrow, not Wednesday, I don't know."

"Oh?" said Anton, sitting up, staring. "Is there anything I should know?"

"Eh," said Oswaldo. He paused. "A matter of certain decisions," he said, with what sounded like effort.

"Decisions," repeated Anton. He wondered how to phrase the question. "But you will be . . . proceeding with the villa?"

"Eh," said Oswaldo again, adding nothing. "Better if I speak to you later. I'll call. So very sorry. I'll call the day after tomorrow. *Tutto bene?*"

Anton made a consenting noise and replaced the receiver in despair.

So. Either Signore Manin had lost the building funds, the contacts, the heart, or he had chosen. And he preferred his Vera and whatever she had done. As Anton had listened to Oswaldo's words, he'd chewed his tongue to keep the weak question from leaping out. Is it her? Just tell me. You like hers more? Just tell me. Tell me! I can bear it.

He could not bear it at all. Presumably he would be paid, as agreed; he'd already been paid part. But his villa! He saw it so clearly it was an agony, shimmering over there on the water. He swallowed some coffee, felt his heart pound inside his robe, and swallowed a little more. He should not drink any more coffee. He should get up, go out.

Yes, well, why not just pack.

He put the cup in the sink and said to himself: What is the matter with you? Why leap to such conclusions? Pull yourself together.

He went into the bathroom, dropped his robe, and stepped into the shower. For a moment he stood there, the water not turned on, and looked down at his body. He had almost forgotten it. It looked lonely down there, long and thin. He touched his chest, his sad little nipple. But with the shock of water came the sense of Josephine, and he shut his eyes to the stream.

Everything was corroding. That rusting ring inside—it scraped his ribs, scratching when he breathed.

All his designs scattered upon the water, his wife spinning wild, out of reach.

Anton left the apartment and walked hard and fast. Lights and banners were strung across Garibaldi, confetti lying all over the ground. Where the road met the bridge, a huge inflatable fun park had been erected, and children were whizzing down a pink rubber slide. A little princess being pushed in a pram looked up at him with dark eyes as she passed.

He walked to San Marco and stopped, amid the crowd, staring at the fantastic columns. Like flesh, this *verde antico* and rose marble, with cold liquid depths. Suddenly it seemed to embody it all, all the things Anton longed for. He placed both palms upon a porphyry column and squeezed shut his stinging eyes.

He walked on and on, catching sight of himself in windows, wild-eyed, his gray coat flying open. The air smelled of burnt sugar, tobacco, and coffee, and in the windows were stockings, small purple artichokes, fur hats, and hanging masks. He crossed the Accademia bridge and walked to the architecture bookshop on the corner.

And there that *woman* actually was, reaching for a book! Anton saw her through the window and nearly started to laugh. Well, where else would she be? No doubt she kept up with it all much better than he did. He'd noticed she wore no rings on her hands. Well then, she had no distractions.

He went in and moved carefully through the aisles, touching a book here and there, eyes down, until he was in the next row. He did not know what he was going to do. He wanted to ask her but could not bear to. There emanated from her an air of intensified value, success; he could feel it a shelf away. Yes, she had that look of someone who has just won a job, someone who has just been made more substantial. He took down a book and stared at it blankly. He had no idea what he was doing. From behind, her shape was hourglass, her coat belted tightly at the waist. Nice coat. Expensive. She'd probably just bought it. She was poring over a book, dark hair falling in her face; she blew it back and returned the book to its shelf, tapping it into place with each finger in turn as if playing the flute. Without seeing him she headed for the door but stopped. She looked down at the magazines and quickly bent down and picked one. Chewing her lower lip, she hurried through the pages until she found what she wanted, near an Absolut ad, and smiled.

But then she must have sensed him there. She looked up, her eyes in her pale face a black glare, and they both straightened and nodded. Anton stepped forward and put out his hand. "Good luck," he said, with dignity. No matter which way things went, it would surely be correct.

She flushed, took his hand, murmured, "Thank you." But as Anton briefly touched her hand, he found himself startled, as if he'd breathed something unexpected.

She returned the journal to its place and left, but he stood there a moment, off-balance. Then he snatched the magazine and flicked to the page she'd been on, hurried through the tiny print, found her name. *Vera—Vera Ponto.* So *that* was it. He knew she'd been familiar; he *knew* he'd read something recently somewhere about someone named Vera.

But then he realized. Gallery listings. It took a moment to understand.

She was not an architect.

Slowly, slowly, the image appeared before his eyes: that aquatic blue jungle, that floating pink form. All at once he streamed blinding light.

Anton hurried home, the long, long way, nearly leaping from the boat. When he reached his building, he took the stairs at a gallop and, once inside, opened his book, found the page, the blue jungle, the pink arm. With an X-Acto blade he pried it free.

Yes, by god, Vera Ponto!

Oh, but once again, Josephine.

And whether Vera Ponto was an artist or not, Oswaldo was still putting him off.

The moment Max woke, he knew it for certain. The weather had changed, and spring was here, waking things, making things move; Lucinde's time was up. She would have to make a decision.

He went out for breakfast to celebrate his decisiveness and to give himself courage. The early-morning streets were empty, the air already heavy and warm. He bought a cup of coffee at the corner store and watched a woman come in wearing her robe and slippers, her face still creased by a pillow. She looked at him with eyes clouded by sleep and last night's rum and mascara; he fixed the lid on his coffee and left. Then he bought some beignets and climbed up to the levee, where he sat on the bench he'd once sat on with Lucinde, and stared out at the river.

The water was muddy, and a ferry was making its way over, not yet at that middle point that always seemed so precarious. On the other shore he could see Algiers, where he had not yet been and whose name both pleased him and seemed foreign, as if the river were a sea. He said it to himself slowly, Algiers.

When Max got home, he listened to the Cajun station while cleaning the ballroom. He tilted the bottomless chairs against the mantelpiece so that he could sweep the floor and put all his shoes and stray books in a row upon the table. Max had two pairs of new shoes, but still there were far more old ones, outweighing. Plain, ordinary, hoofing old shoes, with worn-out soles and knotted laces that looked as if they'd been dragged in the mud. Old shoes, London shoes. He'd walked in them for years.

Had Therese been begging him for something when she did what she did upstairs? When she came down to the door with her stricken eyes? He had looked at her sometimes, and touched her hair, and not known what to do.

Just after two Max called Lucinde. The sky was bright but full of thunderous clouds, and by the time she answered, it was already raining.

"Good afternoon," he said firmly, despite the giddiness that always threatened when he heard her voice.

"Hello," she said. "Hello."

He overcame his weakness and went on. "I've decided, Lucinde, that I can no longer bear it."

There was a silence, and then she said, very slowly, "Well, *well*," just as she had that first time, when he first arrived. "My goodness," she said, sighing, and he imagined he could see her stretch out a long, plump leg. "I was so afraid of this. But of course it was to be expected."

Max was holding the receiver with both hands, pacing an arc at the full length of the cord. He stopped short, facing a wall, and noticed a crack that hadn't been there before.

"We'll have to do something about that, then, won't we?" she said.

"Yes," Max said, "we will."

"Napoleon's, where we didn't go last time?"

On her sixth visit it became clear. Before Doctor Gare had switched off his screen, before he'd even peeled off his gloves. Josephine lay on the table, waiting. He didn't say a word. But at last he rolled back on his stool, and when he looked at her, she knew.

There was nothing at all inside her, no hope. She fell back on the table and laughed, staring up at the freezing Alps.

"Josephine," said Doctor Gare, embarrassed. He stood up, looked down at her, and put his hands in his large white pockets, sunlight glancing from his glasses. But again she laughed; she heard herself. She got up from the table and stood a moment, naked and careless, then sauntered to the dressing room and stepped in, out of sight.

So the last little egg had come and gone, tumbling far away.

Doctor Gare was saying something. "It's true there is such a phenomenon, even among young women like you. A sort of premature termination. But it's also true"—he cleared his throat—"that it could just be psychological. Josephine," he said then gravely. "You can always hope."

What to do but laugh? Bubbles of it welled up like those Mississippi water bubbles, rolled together, tumbled upward, burst at last from her throat.

She left his office and walked home along Saint Charles. It was already warm; one of the early parades was coming. She waited with a few other people under the live oaks. A float wobbled down the street, and from it women in tiaras and T-shirts tossed out little soaps and shampoos. When it started raining, she walked home.

It rained that night and all the next day. Water streamed down the windows, wet leaves slapping against the panes. Warm rain slanted sideways into the porch, and she had to hurry out to drag the sodden cat litter farther into shelter. There were large wet circles on the living-room ceiling; she placed kitchen bowls underneath and waited to hear the crack, the house collapsing to the oceanic sky. The cat retreated under the sofa and lay there looking out with wide eyes; the little dog sat tense on a chair.

While the rain poured down, mildew grew up. Along the walls beneath the windows, by the porch doors, and in the closet as well, it crept up, pale green, and though she brushed it away, it returned, filming the sheaths of dry-cleaned clothes, powdering the shoes. It could be smelled everywhere, not just in the closets but in the kitchen cabinets as well. Moisture fogged Anton's framed prints; even the bedsheets were damp.

In the morning, when the phone rang, Josephine opened her eyes but lay still. Like turning off the lights on Halloween so no children would ring the bell. No one home.

But no one is home.

How could you not have seen that, Anton?

All around her the red line of those charts wavered on blithely like the sea. In the sea the deeper water was colder and less salty, rolling slowly along the floor. The telephone cables were down there, too, all the words rushing invisibly through them, eels moving by. Those female eels with overgrown eyes, trying to see in the dark as they made their long way up the Mississippi. It took years. And then all the way downriver again, ten or twenty years later. To meet their mates waiting in the Gulf, to swim to the Sargasso, to die. They felt, she'd read, like velvet.

After a time the phone rang again, and Josephine tried to picture Anton, in Venice. She shut her eyes and put out her hand, because all she wanted to do was touch him, not have to speak or tell.

They met at a place on the Rio Marin, a single room with a wide smooth bar and little tables of red Verona marble that looked fresh and fleshy, not bleached pale as it always became in the sun. Lach had made a point to be on time, even early, and he had already had two caffè corretti, leaning into the bar with one arm stretched across it, rubbing his finger on the cool stone. A ceiling fan stirred the air; the floor was made of terrazzo with a long, branching crack. He had no clear idea of what he would say, but little surges kept rolling from his nervous stomach to the back of his throat. He was about to abandon the coffee and order a prosecco when the bartender glanced up, and Vera came in, crimson lake on her lips, he noted, and that ridiculous hat.

He smiled, felt a sudden disorder, coughed, and, gesturing sheepishly to excuse himself, hurried through the curtain to the w.c., where he heard her order a glass of prosecco with her awful accent, and he found that an excellent sign—festive! As Lach washed his hands, he was briefly surprised by the starkness of his cheekbones in the mirror, by the debauched look of his eyes. When he emerged, he signaled for a prosecco, too, maneuvered her to his favorite table, and sank onto the banquette. She placed her glass on the stone.

"So!" he said brightly.

She looked at him. "So."

He smiled, took a sip, put a hand secretly to his stomach. "I hope your work's been going well."

She glanced at the mural behind him. "Yes."

Lach drew a circle on the table with his finger. "My favorite table," he said, "because of this." It was a tiny embedded white fossil of a fish, which he touched fondly as she peered at it. "There's another one over there. But that one's harder to see."

She glanced over, anyway, then returned her eyes to him.

"You know I used to collect fossils," he said, the last word slipping into his glass. She was taking a sip, too, and the sight of her bottom lip through the glass was unnerving.

"No," she said flatly. "You didn't."

Lach laughed. "You're right. My brother did. What would I want with fossils?"

He looked at her hand resting upon the red table, at the fine meandering green veins. He could hardly see her eyes; they were shadowed, marbly dark and milky. "So, *Vera*," he said. He felt his mouth bunch up and nearly giggled. "Vera, we really must talk."

"Yes." She nodded. "I know." Her fingertip traced the red patterns in the marble and stopped just short of the fish.

Lach had to begin. He took a breath, shook his head. "Vera, I'm sorry."

She nodded absently, as if she hadn't quite heard.

"I said," he said, "I'm sorry."

"What?"

"What I mean," said Lach, "is that I'm very, *very* sorry. About everything." He found himself fumbling for her hand.

She looked at his hand upon hers. "What do you mean?"

"What do you think?" He laughed a little wildly.

"I don't get it." Her hand slipped away.

"I mean"—he tried again—"it was a mistake."

"What?"

"That time I wanted," he said.

"What?"

"That *time* I wanted," he said again. "It's over."

She shook her head as if to clear it. Then she took a last sip of her drink, replaced the glass carefully on the table, gave him what seemed an unfathomable look, and drew an envelope from her bag. She slid it across to him.

Lach looked at the envelope blankly. The bar seemed to grow loud. After a moment he opened it.

Then the whole thing took less than an hour. As she spoke and he stared at the lawyer's words, words like *common law* and *five years* and *utterly unremunerated*, the room behind Vera, the wide bar, her face, everything seemed to float, all but the pale little fish by his finger. Until at a certain point he felt his own voice coming to life inside, moving through his throat, emerging high and thin. He felt his eyes blink over the clear glass, he felt his dry lips move, trying and trying to say something, until at last the effort was too much, he did not have a chance, it was clear, and he let himself drift with the rest of the room. And then sometime or other, Vera left, Vera left with his little pink house.

After Max called and they arranged to meet, Lucinde stayed home, moving calmly from one room to the other, then bathing. He expected her tonight at eight; he expected her decision. It all felt so familiar.

She sat in the bath and looked at herself, moved her hands through the water. Drawing soap bubbles over her chest, she fashioned them into a décolletage. At the far end of the bath she let her toes poke out from the bubbles, the rest of her hidden in froth. How many years ago had it been, anyway? At least half her life. If she'd been, what, sixteen, seventeen? Her mother had so loved that dress: Lucinde could feel her mother's hands on her back, fastening the tiny clasps. But where was all that, Lucinde wondered, and when? It seemed—somehow, it did not seem possible that it was only seventeen or eighteen years ago. It must have been many more than that, a hundred years, at least. Surely this sort of thing didn't happen these days. Although of course it had all been *proper*. Honey, her mother had whispered to both their faces in the mirror, you know he's just always *adored* you. Still, to this day, she could not see that man's face, only the pinkness, those strangely defined teeth. And what had happened afterward, after the party in the garden, her mother's wandering wet eyes, her father's handshakes and toasts, and her standing there fixed in that dress? Lucinde sat up in the tub. She just could not remember. Some sort of white blur, like the dress itself, its collar all bubbling with lace, its skirts all slippery satin. She could not even remember getting out of that dress. She looked down at herself in the bathtub and laughed. No, she simply could not remember at any moment ever getting out of that dress.

But here she was. And she did not have it on. There were certain disasters, chemical disasters or fires, when clothes were melted onto the skin, taffeta burning into flesh.

Lucinde got out of the tub, dried herself, and rubbed lotion all over her body, lingering. Very slowly she put on her clothes. As if it were that slow, slow ritual all over again. Everything felt dreamy. She touched a wall of her house before leaving, smudging her knuckle white.

She wanted to get to Napoleon's before Max, she really did, it was important: to have just half an hour in the world, among noise, so that she could make the transition. But he might want to get there early himself; that was the kind of thing he would do. So she had to outdo him and leave open an hour. The streets were dark but full of people, the Mardi Gras crowds already in town; the parade that night must already be over. Which was it tonight? Not one of the good ones. She went into Napoleon's, chose a table by the window, and waited to pass into the conversation.

Sacred conversation, silent conversation. She looked around the room, which really was not so unlike a church, if you tried very hard. The old floor was dirty, as were the glasses.

When Max came in, he didn't see her at once, so she sat and watched him. He moved well, she thought, in a foreign place; he took up the right amount of room. There was something so *living* about him, engaged. With that mobile, lined face, those pale blond waves, those hands and knees moving, responding. He has no idea at all, she thought; he does not know how well he does things, how convincing and real he is. He saw her then and had a reaction that moved through him visibly until it reached his mouth and he laughed. He went to the bar and brought them both drinks.

"Maxwell," she said. "Maximilian."

He took her hand; his was dry and warm. They toasted each other and sipped. Outside the window, people moved by in loud groups, carrying go cups and beads.

"So there was a parade tonight?" he said.

She shrugged. "I forget which."

"The important ones—?"

"Start next week."

She was going to continue, but they both fell silent.

"So," he said then.

So, it was time.

"So," she said softly. She cleared her throat and saw his eyes fall to her neck as she swallowed. "So, Maximus. I think you'd like to know something."

"I would," said Max. He was sitting up straight.

Things became vague to Lucinde at the oddest moments. As if they actually went far away, or became blurred or something, difficult to take in. She gazed at her drink. She looked up again. Max was still sitting there. He did not move, his hands latched together, eyes nervous and concerned upon her.

She looked away; she nearly laughed. It was starting to rain again.

"Well," she said again, "Maximilian. The answer seems to be . . . no."

Something seemed to go through him.

She shook her head. "I'm sorry." But she seemed to be laughing or crying, a tear flying free like a spark.

"No to everything?" he whispered. "Nothing?"

She nodded.

He waited a moment and then said, "But why?"

"Because," she began, and stopped. "Because the whole thing is so—" but it was too mortifying to say, just too comical and repellent a thing actually to have in her mouth.

"The whole thing is so what?"

She laughed again; she could not help it. "Implausible," she managed to say, knowing that it would mean nothing. "Hard to fathom." She tried again. "I just can't . . . afford it."

"Afford it?" he said. "I don't understand."

She shut her eyes. He took her hand, and now his was cold.

"But it has nothing to do with you," she said.

"Nothing to do with me?"

"Of course not."

He studied her. "You mean that."

She tried to smile.

"You mean, it would be the same with anyone?"

She nodded.

He stared at her. "You mean, you will never be with anyone."

She nodded again.

"But, Lucinde," he said softly, "I don't understand. You deny yourself—consolation."

He made it so simple. She could not answer. Her eyes, she knew, were wet.

"But are you lost?" he whispered. "Lucinde?"

She didn't speak as he studied her with those optimistic eyes. Then he was silent, his face fallen into long, sad lines as he looked down at his drink. His hands lay lifeless on the table. She folded her own in her lap.

After a time he turned to her. "Well then," he said. He tried to smile. Then he took her hand and kissed the palm hard, put down too much money, and left.

She sat without moving after he'd gone, the puddles outside reflecting red light.

So, was she?

Perde.

That evening Josephine did not turn on the lights. Ever since dusk people had been moving up the street to Saint Charles for the parade, walking not just on the sidewalk but on the street and the neutral ground. Josephine watched them stream by from the front porch, and when she leaned over the balustrade, she could see the crowd at the top of the street, black against the streetlights, waiting. She went back inside and walked down the dark hall. Better not to turn on the lights; more roomy.

At the end of the hall, in the kitchen, the cold light spilling from the open door of the fridge made the dark seem even darker; the glass was smooth in her palm as she poured. She looked down at the glinting liquid and poured a little more. Then, with the live oak leaves rustling at the window and the crowd up the street stirring, excited, she shut her eyes and took a long swallow and felt the cool heat spread through her. She opened the kitchen porch door and went out, hand on the rough wooden balustrade, the gentle breeze in her hair, in her clothes, breathing the muggy smell of the Mississippi; already she could hear the black marching band playing hard and fast with its bright brass instruments and drums. She finished her glass, went in, and poured another, and as she swallowed, she felt deep inside the first loosening, the first sweet melting into that softness, that black.

The parade went by, and Josephine heard it as she moved from room to room, from the front porch back to the kitchen, going from window to window. She touched the dark walls and felt the long cracks that weren't really cracks but dry rivers. At some point she sat in the living room, or maybe it was the bedroom, for a moment she wasn't sure, and stirred her drink dreamily with a finger. Dry rivers, floats, Anton's villa. She remembered something she was sure she'd been trying to remember for hours. Something to do with the water spider, something she'd once upon a time learned. It built a little chamber of air to live in underwater, busily pulling air from above, bubble by bubble, slipping each bubble into the chamber until it was big enough and the spider moved in, into its miraculous house.

Suddenly she thought: Anton. She giggled.

She got up again and roamed, fingers trailing along the walls. Were her fingertips leaving dry rivers? She poured a fresh glass and swallowed a fresh mouthful, shutting her eyes and letting the liquid run cool into the hot caverns of her head. Was she still in the kitchen? She opened her eyes, but it was dark even then. No, this wasn't the *kitchen*, of course not. She'd already left the kitchen. This was the *bath*room. She sat down on the rim of the tub.

And here's where I injected myself full of black holes.

They're not really black holes, you know, just what I call them.

I know, I know, I know. Not black *holes*, not really. I know. And besides, I didn't really inject them. They were in me all along.

What do you mean?

Oh, you know what I mean! As aphids are born with baby aphids already inside them, and inside those babies are still smaller babies, I was born already with nothing.

You could put a pin in my skin and I'd pop!

Josephine got up and went to the sink, which she held with one hand, trying to find her reflection. Her face was lit by the streetlight, so that dark greenish shadows stretched from her nose and fell away from her chin. She squinted and focused, very close, until she found the black holes in her eyes.

So you *see*, she thought to the pair of black holes, you were there inside me all along! There was never any chance at all. What a silly idea it had been. She could have told him right from the start. He should have known, in fact, right from the start. Wasn't the evidence there?

She couldn't remember, suddenly, what. She fixed upon the black points again. Yes. The black holes. Oh yes. Funny how they ran right through her. Like hollow tubes running in from her eyes, so that everything could spill straight out, down the drain.

She went down the hallway to the bedroom, bumping softly against the walls. It was so dark; she tried opening her eyes wider to see if that would help, but it made no difference at all. She patted for her dresser, for the drawer; not the top drawer, the one beneath. There. After a moment she found the box, and then, with a little fumbling, she'd opened it to the row of glass eggs.

Josephine went back to the bathroom with the box and stood swaying at the sink. As she loosened one little vial from its plastic pincers, it was like Easter, small hands groping behind bushes, in the grass, for the sweet surprises. The vial came free and lay lightly, a translucent egg in her palm.

She shook her head sadly. Oh, she thought, you just couldn't help, could you.

It snapped very easily between her fingers; a little glass and liquid dropped to the floor. The second one broke easily, too, tiny slivers of glass glinting like ice at her feet.

The telephone seemed to be ringing. It was always ringing. She paid no attention; there were still seven vials. But it rang and rang, and at last, after she'd crushed the last one, she hurried back down the dark hall, that blackness already nudging at the edges of her mind.

What?

Time slipped, or something; it seemed she'd already answered. She was already standing there with the receiver in a sticky hand. Anton seemed already to know.

"All right," he said. She heard that clearly. Then he seemed to be waiting, and she wasn't certain why. "Are you going to tell me?"

"Tell you? What?" The receiver slipped in her hand, and she held it away and looked at it. He was saying something, his voice small and urgent. But his voice was so very far away, she could actually just hang up. She lowered the receiver to its cradle, but then she remembered—Anton!—and brought it back to her ear.

"Yes?" she said politely.

"Yes?" He was silent, the meter ticking. "What do you mean, yes? What do you think I want you to tell me?" Then he said, more softly, "What's happened?"

Josephine felt brass rings close around her and tried to remember what he meant. "Oh that," she said, vague. "Didn't you know?"

"Didn't I know what?"

"You know. That I didn't."

"Didn't? What?"

She shrugged hopelessly, exaggeratedly, in the darkness. "You know. I just didn't."

"I don't know. Didn't what? Didn't do it, you mean? This time? Do the shots?"

She held the phone steady a moment, and things seemed to grow clear. "Right," she whispered. Her breath moved into the plastic device in her hand and rolled like a current through the sea, all the way to him, committing. "Right," she repeated. "I decided—" She opened her eyes wide in the dark. "I *decided*," she said again, emphatic, "I just didn't want to."

He did not answer at once. The meter clicked like the wings of a beetle clicking its deadly signal.

"What you're saying is that you didn't want to do it, after all," he said at last.

She nodded, said nothing, and stared into the long hallway. Didn't, couldn't; she couldn't speak. She wanted a cigarette. She hadn't smoked in years. Opening her mouth, she seemed to feel the dry gray smoke flow from her. She could hear him breathing then, in curious, rough bursts.

After hanging up, Anton stood still for a time in the center of the room. Then he put on his jacket, left the apartment, and, without planning it, walked toward the bottom of the island and over the bridge to Sant'Elena Church. It was early, so the church doors were locked. The grass was overgrown, and the trees were unkempt live oaks. He picked up an acorn, tossed it down, and walked through the trees to the water.

Had he wanted more than he should have?

He stared out at the Lido, the island floating upon the morning mist. Near him the water jostled, and he gazed at it, at the reflected colors, at the ripples of light, and wondered if this would happen to him always, if he would always be haunted. Because there again that old image was. The soaked white shirt, the floating tie, the dead hand with its sodden cigarette. As if the decision to die hadn't even really been made, just quietly stepped into, shrugging.

Anton turned away from the water and walked back through the trees, up toward San Francesco della Vigna. Banners were stretched across the *calle*; music was playing from shops; pink and green and yellow confetti lay sticky on the ground. Anton went into the church, into the darkness, and stood before a childlike Madonna, behind whose throne waves seemed to be breaking. For a time he stood still, in the dim, dusty nave, feeling himself in the emptiness.

He used to watch her as she slept, watch the tip of her tongue moving behind her teeth like something just breaking the surface of the sea and then sounding, down.

Out of the church, back in the bright morning light, Anton walked along the *calle* and went over the bridge, following the route to San Zanipolo. A man in a wig and red velvet tails walked briskly past, carrying a briefcase. Anton went into the airy vault of the church, sat in a pew, and shut his eyes.

After a time he got up and walked slowly along the south aisle, light falling in the huge, airy space. He stood before the Bellini polyptich, Saint Sebastian full of arrows, beautiful Saint Christopher striding through water, veins branching down the muscle of his arm, the tiny child safe upon his shoulder. Farther up the aisle was a marble baby with glossy knees; then a stone sphinx with polished stone breasts.

Her body, her head, he just could not find his way.

He went around to the north aisle, to all the sepulchral monuments. Stopping before one, he crossed his arms and stared up at the marble bones.

It could have been anyone. She'd said it herself, with her black tongue. It didn't have to be you, you know. It could have been anyone else.

Anton felt himself trembling and dug his nails into his palms to stop. But still he trembled, as if something inside were loosening, breaking.

He was in the center of the huge building; no one else was there. Light fell in the high windows, infusing the volumes of old air, dropping upon the worn stones. It seemed that the floor gently rocked, as if the stones had been laid not upon piles in the mud, but directly upon the sea.

It was all, Anton thought, just too difficult.

A pigeon soared through the vault, reached a window, and settled. He gazed up at the window, at the brightness of sky flaring at the stone frame, dissolving inside and out. And somewhere in his mind another window appeared, a window with an old man seated nearby, a man with longing gray eyes. It was a painting; it had leaned against a wall at Signore Manin's; it was a painting of Manin himself. Anton had not taken much notice. But now he saw: a painting by Vera.

He could see her shadowed eyes as she absorbed what she saw, see her hand behind her back already imagining what it would do.

It was noon; the bells began to ring, and the sacristan appeared. Anton went outside to brightness and noise in the *campo*, where pop music blared from speakers on a platform. Little cave-children, wearing fake-fur pelts and shaking plastic clubs, were running in circles and dancing while their mothers stood by, applauding. He leaned against the wall of the church and watched the children, their little bare shoulders and running knees. And for the first time he allowed a blind to fall over his eyes.

He thought, Maybe I don't want any of that anymore.

He thought, Maybe I want something new.

Max signed all the papers in the emerald-green building near the warehouse district, and then he went with the keys to find the rental car. It was emerald-green, too, small and bright, like an insect. He walked around it, inspecting, put a foot to a tire, and finally opened the door and got in. He hadn't driven for he did not know how long. He hadn't driven on this side of the road. The cigarette smell, the warm vinyl; he rolled down the windows and turned on the radio, which blasted loud, and with just a touch of gas Max lurched from the lot and was seventeen, and girls were new again.

It was still morning, and he'd have the car until the same time tomorrow. He drove east. At least it seemed to be east; with the river's bendings, it was hard to keep track. Downriver, at any rate. A map flapped on the seat beside him, held down with a guidebook. He drove through the Eighth Ward, then the Ninth, and he knew the river was somewhere, snaking along to his right. There were things worth seeing, his guidebook said, and as he drove, he glanced now and then at the fluttering pages and tried to follow the descriptions of sights with one finger, while he looked for the sights themselves, quickly to left or right, the bright green car flying over the ruined roads. The sun was in his eyes, and already, even on the first of March, he could imagine the place as it would be in the summer, with hot, fallen houses and roads cracking like mud.

The first of March? Had it actually been four months, then? Four months of this pointless pursuit?

Max drove on, flinching at traffic to his left, keeping his eyes near the curb for protection. As old men drove at night, looking for the white line to steer their precarious course. Was he an old man? It seemed that he had always been an old man, or somehow either sixteen or ancient, somehow lost in between. He did not know how to do things.

Somewhere was the Saturn Bar, somewhere was the big pink Cadillac, but Max could not see any of it. The steamboat houses, too, by the levee, he had thought he'd like to see—he'd even underlined them in the book—but that street had already passed. Everything came so much faster than he'd thought.

Now he crossed into Saint Bernard Parish, and the city surfaces began to fall away. The road glided around to the right, away from the highway and progress, toward water. A narrow canal appeared alongside the road, a thread of water between slopes of green grass. On it floated water lilies, empty trash bags, soda cans.

So had Therese really been pleading when she stood at the door? Had he just made a mistake?

Max drove on, past other sights that were listed in the guidebook—a church shaped like a boat, for instance, and the Isleño museum—but he could not find them, even when finally he'd had enough and pulled over and carefully examined the map, even when he doubled back in a fit of determination and slowly retraced his route. There seemed to be no connection at all between the book and this terrain. Like a desert that shifted, its topography changing.

Without his noticing, the skinny little thread of water at his right seemed gradually to have widened, spread, slowly to have become a bayou. Max found himself driving past fishing huts on stilts, men and boys in old hats and boots who carried buckets and looked up as he passed.

What was he doing here?

Then the road came to an end. There was no more ground, so the road simply stopped. That little canal had swollen and spread and finally stretched over everything, and Max had not even noticed. He was in a small flat parking lot of dirt and broken oystershells, with tall grasses at the edges, where the water began. Boats were moored nearby. To all sides were water, bayou, sky. THE END OF THE WORLD, said a sign before him. It was starting to rain again.

When she had finally stood at the door with her bags, she'd looked just as she always looked, so that he could not understand how it had happened, when he had disappeared from her eyes.

But didn't you love me first? he said.

She looked at him, and as he watched, helpless, her eyes filled again. She didn't speak.

I'm sorry, he had murmured, his hand reaching for her hair but returning then to his side, to his pocket.

Rain was streaming down the windshield. He couldn't find the wipers. He rolled up the windows and turned off the engine and sat there in the quiet sound of rain.

He thought again of the wild little pigs that had once run through German forests.

He had known it was foolish to move here, on this quest. It was just that there had to be something of interest, in all the years that would come and go, to jolly himself along.

———————

After a while Max roused himself. He had rented the car for twenty-four hours; it would be wasteful not to use it. He smoothed open the map and consulted the guidebook. Maybe he'd go to Algiers.

It was pouring again in New Orleans, too much rain for the pumping stations to manage, the ground already soaked. Rain streamed down so that windows on all four sides of the yellow house seemed liquid, leaves slapping the panes. In the back and front gardens, water sheeted the ground until only the tips of the grass blades showed, and then even they were submerged, and the ground was all pool reflecting sky, while the sky was all water.

Josephine had woken with little cuts in her palms. Bits of glass lay on the floor, crunching beneath her slippered feet. With toilet paper she wiped up the slivers in the sink and splashed the rest down the drain.

Money and eggs and inky babies, swirling down the drains. No wonder such lush algae grew there, swaying in the darkness.

She looked at herself in the mirror. Trash.

Droplets of rain were streaming down the window, joining briefly to form larger drops, then trailing off alone again. Josephine leaned her forehead against the glass, exhaled slowly, and tried to imagine herself other. How did people do things? How was it, between the first impulse to lift a foot and place it somewhere farther, how was it that the impulse itself did not fly forward to the logical, futile end and fizzle like a snapped electric wire,

burn to nothing, so that there was nothing at all to stand on? Because everything ended up nothing; there was no getting around
that. She could look at her hands and imagine them gone; look at
this house and imagine it gone; consider the things that one might
do, and see them, years later, forgotten. And that constant running
of her thoughts down a drain she just could not prevent.

Laughing was easier. Standing before Anton and just laughing, giddy, throwing up her hands, throwing back her head.

So, she knew she had never wanted it.

That wasn't true.

Of course it was.

She laughed. Of course it was true. She did not want anything. She could not see how.

How do I tell you I'm sorry, Anton?

Rain rivered down the street; it swirled and eddied at the gutters
until they could hold no more, and then the water rose up the
curbs, sloshing and deep. Lost dogs splashed down the sidewalks,
confused by all the drowned scents, bedraggled, pausing at corners to smell something familiar, then splashing on hopefully,
farther from home.

Josephine gave the cat and the little dog extra bowls of dinner
before she left the house. Rivers were lapping up over the curbs
as she ran to the K&B, where soggy paper bags were laid on the
floor. She selected a nice tall dark bottle and, with her package
tucked under her arm, went out again and got on the streetcar.

Water, water, Le Flottant. The whole place seemed to be floating; even the streetcar hydroplaned. Floating houses, floating
cars, floating live oaks and dead palm trees. Were they likely to
come back to life after freezing? Discreetly she twisted off the top
of her bottle and took a private sip.

The streetcar reached the last stop, downtown, and everyone got off. Some people had given up on their shoes, so Josephine took hers off, too, and splashed barefoot over the sidewalk.

Water, water, everywhere. She took another drink. She did not take the bottle out of the bag but held the paper close to the neck so that it was concealed. Although so silly, she thought, when here they have go cups and even those drive-through daiquiri places. No cause at all ever to panic! She saw a sign for the ferry to Algiers: straight ahead. She thought of Charon oaring over the underworld river; then she thought of Mercury. Wasn't he the one who took you? Mercury was the way in, through the mirrors: all you did was dive.

She walked straight ahead for several blocks. Streamers ran across the street: purple, gold, and green, slapping. At least now the rain had stopped, the streets shining wet. When she reached the ferry, a few cars were already boarding, and the smell of the river was strong and cool.

The upper deck was empty, and the whole thing vibrated as it idled. When it left the dock and pushed out into the Mississippi, it seemed to be struggling, dogged. Josephine stood holding on to the railing, but her hands vibrated so violently she sat down instead on the deck, looked around, and had another drink.

The ferry approached the middle of the river, the lights of New Orleans far away to one side, those of Algiers to the other. She stood up, unsteady, and looked over the edge, into the roiling water. Deep, she knew; very deep. *A forty-five-foot channel from Head of the Passes to Baton Rouge.* Forty-five feet! That was very deep. That was herself times just over eight.

And down there all the female eels were gliding along, silent, down to the Gulf to find their mates, then the long way home to the Sargasso. She knelt and placed her empty bottle carefully on the deck. She made sure her shoes were neatly beside it. Then she put both hands on the railing.

The boat had reached the middle of the river and was beginning to turn against the stream. The city lights and the darkness wheeled around. She put one foot on the bottom rail.

Once, when she was small, she'd been on a raft at the beach, a blue raft with yellow edges and a white cord. The other children were older, and as she kicked to keep up with them, the current began to pull at her legs, without her even noticing. It pulled at her calves, pulled at her thighs, began gently loosening her from the raft, and still she noticed only that it seemed a little harder to hold on. The current pulled at her hips, slipped around her stomach, and then the raft, instead of being under her stomach, seemed to be only under her chest. Then it was not even under her chest, just clutched in her hands, and suddenly, somehow, it slipped right away, and she held only the cord. The others by now were far, their heads small across the choppy water. And without its making any sense at all, the cord too slipped out of her fingers, and she had nothing, she was pulled away, water sloshing into her mouth.

Maybe, she suddenly thought, maybe I don't want this.

She struggled to hold on to the wet rail.

But already something was happening. That blackness, coming over her eyes. Where were her hands? Where were her feet? She tried to grip the slippery railing, but now the boat revolved as it moved forward, so that all the city and Algiers and the long dark river itself seemed to spin around her, and Josephine could not hold on to the rail, and she slipped, she lost her balance.

Max shut his eyes and breathed the wet night air, his mouth slightly open. He was at the top of the ferry's stairwell, having climbed up from where the cars were parked to watch Algiers approaching. He'd driven his rental car all day. To the End of the World and back again, then along the river to see some plantations, and he was exhausted. His face kept shuddering and stretching with yawns, and what he really wanted to do was sleep, fall forward, shoes on. But a twenty-four-hour rental was a twenty-four-hour rental; there'd be no chance for Algiers in the morning, and he wouldn't think of wasting the time.

He opened his eyes to the windy darkness. The boat must have reached the middle, because he could feel it start that laborious turning as it continued to plow forward. Exciting! Enough to wake him right up. The lights of New Orleans, the lights of Algiers: all of it seemed to swing around as the boat began to swivel. He put out his arms to enjoy the dizziness and opened his mouth to the breeze for the thrill.

But then he noticed someone unsteadily climbing the railing. Was that the funny lush?

Just then the engine shifted huge gears, and the whole boat suddenly lurched.

It was raining then in Venice, too; Anton couldn't sleep. At five he finally got up and went out to walk, to think it through. The paving stones were slippery, black, and as he walked, he held his coat close.

The rain was steady, featureless, without thunder or storm. It fell and fell, and as it fell, seawater rose, bubbling through the slits in the granite. At first puddles formed around those slits, but they gradually spread, joining each other, until water covered the passageways and the bubbling was no longer discernible. At San Marco the moored black boats banged and rose, until at last the lagoon spilled over the embankment. Soon a single surface of water stretched from the sea to the city. Buildings seemed to float on it then, buildings of Istrian, *verde antico*, and mottled Verona marble gliding like ships on the seamless sea.

But I can't just give up, thought Anton.

At six-thirty he returned to his apartment, soaked. Just one call, he told himself. One simple call, a clear pipe of air blown between us, her voice.

He picked up the receiver and dialed, then placed his palm against the window and waited, looking out at the lagoon.

A slow ring, the long pause, another ring. He could hear it all the way in New Orleans, the ripples dissolving in the dark of that old wooden house. Another ring, and as he stared out the window, he thought of the ring that had been dropped in the lagoon each year, that sacred golden ring, a promise. Five rings, six, falling into the emptiness. Four more, and it would be over.

The phone was answered.

"Hello?" a man mumbled.

Anton stared at the receiver. The meter clicked. Then he whispered, "Max?"

Finally the rain stopped, and the sky began to clear, clouds rolling over the city, fresh zones of blue tearing open. Oswaldo looked down his stairs at all the new puddles on the floor. Then he put on his boots and walked through them, got into his boat, and drove out to the lagoon.

When he reached the mouth, by Sant'Erasmo, he switched the engine off. The boat rocked, unfamiliarly quiet. Overhead a seagull flew, its form neat and gray against the clear sky. Oswaldo sat in his captain's seat and looked at the water all around him: the sparkling jade surface, the bundled wooden piles, the islands floating on mist. He moved his gaze slowly from the Lido to Le Vignole, to Venice itself.

Once upon a time nothing was here, nothing but tidal waters, grasses, and mud. Everything was brought and constructed. First the sand and the soil and the wooden beams, then the bricks and the tiles for roofs. All of it was painstakingly borne over the water, poured or pounded into the shallows, erected from the mud. Gradually, from a crude little village, a magnificent city was formed, and it was adorned with riches: the slices of porphyry, slabs of Carraran, bending carved caryatids, *grotteschi*; moiré silks, clear white glass, all the damask and velvet; that alabaster ewer with its silver rim, that rock crystal lamp cut like a fish, that golden chalice, that narwhal's carved tooth; and all the gorgeous paintings. Riches and beauty heaped upon the sea!

And here, thought Oswaldo, here where I idle, right here on this tossing green water, once they had constructed their miraculous city, those poor Venetians committed a greater vanity yet. Here they dropped a golden ring into the water each year and took their solemn vows: *Desponsamus te, mare, in signum veri perpetuique dominii*. A hopeful marriage between their precarious selves and the heedless sea.

Oswaldo folded his hands together and sighed. Poor Venice, he thought, poor little men. All the busyness and vainglorious fuss that we make, all for nothing. A day will come when nothing is left, and no one left to see.

Why bother?

He sighed again, his hands stiff and aching. Another boat flew by, with a man and a young boy and a heap of nets. The boy sat eagerly at the prow, his mouth slightly open.

Oswaldo sat rocking in the boat's wake, watching as it skimmed away.

But what else? he thought.

So what, if it's all nothing?

What else can we possibly *do*?

He squinted toward the Lido, beyond it to the stretching sea. Then slowly he turned the boat around and motored back to the busy city.

From the darkness, from the depths, the light seemed very fine and sharp, needling Josephine's eyes, and by then it was too late. She felt the old horror spread through her, fanning out from the ribs. The pain in her head was violent.

She thought, Did anyone see?

It was a thought from years ago, from the time before Anton, a thought no longer relevant. But the thoughts that might be relevant she could not bear to think. She stumbled down the hall to the bathroom, and then everything poured out of her, not just vomit but tears and blood, and it seemed that she was splitting open, blood dripping down her legs and tears from her eyes and mucus from her nose, and she could not hold herself together.

All she could remember was the K&B, the streetcar, the rain. She had just been riding the streetcar, walking in the watery streets. No, there was also the ferry. She remembered getting on the ferry, remembered sitting down by the rail. And then? Something. The dark water, the currents . . . And then? What? Was there someone?

The apartment around her was quiet, the cat stretched in the sun, the dog watching. But all her clothes were on. She looked down at her body. Yesterday's clothes were still on.

She knew she had to call Anton.

She stood by the phone with her eyes shut. But when he finally answered, she saw at once that he knew. He knew all about it, much more than she did.

He spelled it out for her patiently, cold.

"A man was there," he said.

She shut her eyes and didn't answer.

"A man whose name is Max."

Max.

"You do know a Max?"

She nodded. "Yes."

"I thought you did. It was about two o'clock in the morning," he added.

She didn't know what she could say.

"I gather you were asleep," he said.

"I guess, yes."

"Asleep, or something like that."

Neither of them said anything.

"And you probably want me to think nothing happened. Before you fell asleep."

"I don't know," she said, fingertips at her eyes.

"Don't know," he repeated. He was silent a moment. "Josephine, it's too much."

She didn't know what to say. One dirty bare foot curled over the other, and she stared out the window, then stared at the kitchen. There seemed to be a few tiny wings on the floor.

"Most likely the usual happened," he said.

"Well," she said, "if it did, can't you believe that it didn't—"

"Mean anything?"

"Something like that, yes."

She could hear his bitterness, hear that tremble in his hand.

"I've never understood that," he said. "But you hear it so often. It didn't mean anything. If *that* doesn't mean anything, I

don't know what does. Josephine. If you get yourself into that
state, surely it has to mean something."

Josephine looked at Mrs. Mouton's garden. What did *mean*
mean, anyway? The word seemed wrong, its letters and sounds
slipping. Anton was silent, and the telephone ticked between
them, the currents moving over the deep, buried cables. All over
the floor, she now saw, lay tiny wings, glinting in the sun.

"Josephine," he said quietly, "you weren't really up to this,
were you?"

"To what?"

"All of this. You know what I mean. This whole ordinary venture."

These words just seemed beyond her, too bright.

"Well," she said. "I guess not."

"But why didn't you ever say anything?"

Say anything? Say what? She looked at the phone in her hand,
at the garden, then up at the disappearing blue sky.

"Why didn't you say that this just didn't interest you?"

"But I don't even know if that's true."

"I think," he said, "we can both assume it."

The phone calls went on for another few days, sickly and aborted.
Finally Anton said, "I think, Josephine, we need a break."

She repeated the word to herself, in her head, where a watery
noise began at her ears and pulsed behind her eyes. Look at you,
he'd said. You're gold.

"A break," she said.

"A break."

She touched her eyes. An anole was clinging to the window
screen, its slender body nearly translucent. "You know," she began, but it was all too much.

"What?" He waited.

She shut her eyes. "I think you're probably right."

He didn't answer. The watery noise was growing loud, so that she could no longer hear the ticking of the meter, and even her sight seemed affected, a glare.

After a moment he said, "I thought I should tell you, I'm going away."

She laughed. "You already are away."

"From here."

"I don't think it'll make much difference."

"I meant we won't be speaking. For a time."

Then, at some point, she hung up. As she stood in the kitchen, her hand upon the receiver in its cradle, the light streaming into the kitchen seemed to intensify, to bleach the walls and thin them. And for the first time she understood she was alone.

It was like something she could almost remember but not quite, something she could almost taste or name. She left the phone and went into the dining room, it too all filled with light. This felt so strangely familiar. Light rose up from the gold wool rug, Anton's rug, and she realized that it would probably leave, there would probably be a division of things, everything would go floating. She sat. The wicker weave of the chair startled her as it pressed the backs of her legs, so real. She placed her elbows upon the table, Anton's table. It seemed to be leaving already, drifting away. She pressed her elbows harder and latched her hands together and made an effort to keep everything down.

From blocks away, up the street, came the sound of another marching band.

The whole week before Carnivale itself, people in Venice wore masks. They strode through the *calli* arm in arm, their long velvet and silk and polyester capes swinging; they stood on bridges and had their pictures taken; they paused and smoked and tossed confetti, looking complacently out through the eyeholes. This morning there had been a costumed parade in San Marco as Anton walked through, women's bare busts mottled pink in the cold.

Well, of course, he thought as he pulled his bag from the closet. What could I have been thinking.

He folded his clothes carefully and laid them in the bag, rolled up his bright silk ties. For nearly a week he'd felt a sort of white flame in his body, a purifying flame, cold heat.

She'd had no need for him at all.

No, that was wrong; he corrected himself. She'd had only need for him, nothing else. But anyone could have been under that streetlamp. I was invisible.

Or no, again wrong. I was not invisible. I was perfectly visible. But only as something is visible to insects with their compound eyes, which see not what we see but only light, color, whether the object is dangerous or will serve.

He hummed bitterly as he rolled up the tracing paper on his

desk, swept away the shreds of eraser, and took apart the Mayline. He hummed at a pitch that, as he moved about the apartment, grew higher and finer until it was taut. He stopped. He looked down at his trembling hands.

But hadn't it been worth a try?

He had loved her.

He looked at the room around him, all his things packed up; he looked out the window to the glinting jade water. He went over to the terrace door and opened it, and as a gust of cool salt air blew in, a swell rolled through his heart.

Venezia.

The name itself sounded of bottle-green glass, smoky lacework, marble, Cima skies and gold brocade, solid blocks of Istrian stone, sweet *peoci* mussels.

Venezia.

I do not want to leave.

Lunch? she'd said earlier, on the phone. Over here, at my place?

This was after the two had met with Oswaldo, after he'd toasted them both with Bellinis and told them to proceed.

Bands were playing along Garibaldi when Anton strode the familiar route; confetti lay bright on the ground. He whistled harshly through his teeth as he walked to the vaporetto stop. A man on the platform wore a long black cloak and held a scythe, drawing pensively on a cigarette as he studied the timetable.

Her place was next to the Redentore. It was pink.

"You're renting it?" he asked as she opened the door.

She laughed, shrugged, and shook her head before climbing the dark stairs.

His hand lightly touched the plaster wall as he rose. To live here, of all places. Beside the Redentore!

They reached the main floor, the marvelous light, the walls

with their patina of markings. There were only a few pieces of furniture. "You're working on it?" he asked.

"Well," she said, "just look at it."

He did. He paced out a length. "What do you think you'll do?"

"Not sure." She looked a little embarrassed, laughed again, and hurried into the kitchen.

Lucinde stood at the front door of her house, looking out at the street. The warm green haze of Esplanade, the air already heavy and hazy. The crepe myrtle, live oaks, jasmine, palms. She took a deep breath, closed her eyes, and slowly shut the door, the veil of light across the entrance hall disappearing. She stood there a minute, then locked the door and slipped in the little chain. She turned into the bare whiteness of her house. Silently she went to the nearest window and latched it, then to the next one, and latched it, too, then to each of the others.

She was walking very deliberately, looking at the walls, watching her bare feet on the floorboards. Then she was in her favorite room, her most private room, the one with the *trasparente* lighting. She went to the mirror and stood before it, considering herself. The walls of the room reflected behind her were white and peeling, and the porcelain bathtub gleamed. Water slowly filled the bath, clouds of steam rising but not yet fogging the mirror. She stood as far from the glass as one stands from a lover, less than an arm's length away. When she looked in the mirror, she knew it was not just the image of herself that she looked at; it was something much harder to find than that. She took off her clothes, not quickly.

Perde.

She looked over at her bath. Nearly full. It would really be just a matter of willpower, she knew. Of discipline, control.

CARNIVAL

At dawn Vera lay awake in bed, watching the sky gradually lighten. From here in the loft she could see it through the skylight, and again, a little paler, through the window. Carefully, to cause little motion, she drew one hand from under the sheet, then the other. She stretched both arms out before her and looked at them in the dimness.

Masked figured had pushed and shouted through the passageways all day, colorful and loud; traveling bands had piped and beaten their music; people had thrown confetti. There had been parades and shows and parties in the *campi*, but gradually it had grown cold, the light thinning, and then a fog rolled in. It might have crept over from the Veneto or in from the sea, or it might have simply risen, an exhalation of the lagoon itself. But they had decided it was too cold and damp to stay out any longer, so retreated to the small pink house. They could watch the fireworks from there.

But the fog had been thick outside the windows and obscured the city completely; they could see only the dim lantern outside, while moored boats invisibly bumped. After a time, though, there was a muffled boom, and the fog became tinged with rose. Then there was another explosion, and the fog was illuminated gold.

Afterward, a little while ago, when he was already asleep, Vera had wept a little. Silently, with her body rigid, her mouth open and wet on the pillow. But that had gradually subsided. She had turned and lain still on her back, gazing through the darkness at the ceiling.

So you're finally gone now, she thought. You are finally out of me.

In the past weeks there had been terrible phone calls, but at last Lach had come to the house and taken all his things. She had stood watching him from the kitchen, her hand pressed against the doorjamb.

Yet still, still, even tonight, Vera had dreamt about him again. His face looking at hers through blue blades of grass, with that guilty, dissolute smile.

She looked at her arms again in the dimness.

Goodbye, she said in her mind. She waited until she felt nothing.

After a while she stretched and turned to see, in the weak light, this body she had washed up beside, out here in the huge, rocking world.

He slept as Lach had never slept, not abandoned, but with his face like a marble bishop. Vera studied it and guessed he did not even know how fine his face was. A mouth that looked bitter, but she did not think it need be.

She had first liked his coat, and then his smell, and then the trembling of his hands. She decided, after all, that this was enough.

And the woman . . . Vera tried to conjure her from the few words he had said. She understood that he was very far from having ended it but that soon he would. That he would end it because of *her*.

This was a lie, she knew, and she smiled at the ceiling. Well, not altogether a lie, just a sweet little illusion to fend it all off. It could have been almost anyone.

In New Orleans the ragged flambeaux had already passed with their torches, and the young black bands with their dead-set eyes had beaten their drums, beaten the ground with their heels. Now the rivers of people in the darkness waited for the largest float. They surged and pressed on either side as at last it wobbled forward; it was nearly two stories high, its wheels and machinery hidden in decoration and light as it lurched along.

Bacchus! People shouted and waved their arms, hands grasping, eager to catch anything thrown by the costumed krewe. Plastic money, plastic jewels: worthless, but who could care less? It was what everyone wanted! While the others threw coins from the lower deck of the float, Bacchus stood crowned at the top, a rubber snake around his neck. He slowly unwound the snake and held it out to the shouting crowd; he made it squirm as if alive; he threatened to hurl it but then held it back so it became more precious. Meanwhile the plastic coins kept flying, and plastic beads kept spinning in the air, and the crowds on the street screamed and leapt, trying to catch them, their arms straining and reaching in the dark.

Then Bacchus decided to let loose the snake. Slowly, as if stripping, he again drew it free from his neck; he held it, tempting first the crowd to his left, then the crowd to his right. He toyed with it for another moment, whispering to its fanged rubber head. Then suddenly he drew it back and threw, and the snake flew through the air, long and kinking, coiling, uncoiling, as if it were alive. It flew above all the reaching hands, over the heads as people leapt; it flew toward Max and Josephine. A rubber snake, a dime-store snake. The crowd screamed with tension, with excitement. Max found himself breathless, leaping, pushing, and Josephine found herself jumping into the air. Then Max grabbed its rubber head, Josephine snatched its rubber tail, and they fell back together laughing into the crowd, upon the street slippery with plastic coins.

The huge float wobbled on like an ark, upon its waving river. At the corner it turned into Saint Charles and began to make its slow way downtown. It passed the K&B; it passed Louisiana. And there, down a few blocks, in the old yellow house, a darkness seemed to gather, to condense, to lift like smoke from the dead fireplace. It drifted over the moss-covered branches, where the caterpillars were just beginning to chew. It drifted down over the warehouses, over the Quarter, along the levee, to Esplanade. And there at last it sifted down through another shaft, another former fireplace, and into a clean, white, empty room.